A SNAPSHOT OF HOPE

NELIANNE GENNER

FIREFLY HILL PRESS

To our beloved Roxy. You will forever be in our hearts.

CHAPTER ONE

As I walked slowly through the tunnel of bright, blinking lights in the village, an overwhelming feeling of nostalgia swept over me. I gazed out over a sea of illumination and lost myself in the memories of Christmas past.

"Sophia, should we find a spot for you to take your pictures?" Long, curly, red hair obstructed my view.

"Yes, please!"

"When we're finished, you can go back to your happy place," she said in a sarcastic undertone.

"You know me too well, Rae."

Raelyn Taylor was like a second sister to me. Our mutual friend, Kendal, had introduced us roughly six years ago, and we were immediately attached at the hip. We lived in the same small town of Buckingham, Pennsylvania, with our similar interests soaring beyond your typical taste in books, music, and films; the two of us were deeply connected. We were as close as any two women could be, and we supported each other in all aspects of life. I even got along well with her family, which is why I was not the least bit surprised when she asked me to be the maid of honor in her wedding last summer.

I will never forget standing under the archway at the lake on that warm, sunny day taking in the smells of lavender and fresh cut grass. Thankfully, my long blonde hair had been braided into a loose side bun, and my royal blue dress with one side strap stopped three inches above my knee. I remember admiring how angelic she looked in her long, strapless, ivory wedding dress and short floral veil. As the ceremony concluded, the sun made its descent behind the water, and the sky shifted to swirls of purple, orange, and pink. It was a beauty that could never be captured fully by any camera or matched by any other season. Summer was hands down the only time of year I enjoyed more than Christmas.

"Raelyn, let's park ourselves by the white gazebo while we wait for Kendal and her cousin to get here. We can see most of the village from there, and I should be able to get some decent shots for the website." The couple was running fashionably late, as was pretty usual for these types of events. We had to be blending in by the pond in less than ten minutes for the main event.

"I just got the text from Kendal. They are pulling into the parking lot right now and told us to be ready." I could hear Raelyn's voice buzzing behind me. I tended to get deep in the zone with my work, and Christmas lights in the village were always spectacular to photograph.

"Sophia, did you hear me? We have to head over to the pond in a minute."

"Yup, got it!" Her instruction snapped me back to the present, and I slung my camera bag over my shoulder, adjusting the strap around my heavy coat.

We arrived at the pond and stood in place only thirty seconds before Kendal and her cousin, John, and his girlfriend, Kate, approached. Trying to hide in plain sight is a lot trickier than it sounds, but we did our best to stay hidden and look inconspicuous. My camera was ready, and I was overcome with joy.

My heart swelled, and I couldn't help but exclaim aloud, "This is so romantic!"

Immediately, Rae slapped a hand over my mouth. "*Shhhh!*" she hissed and then repositioned her iPhone in their direction to snap some pictures of her own.

John and Kate stood in front of the pond under the tall lamp post with a backdrop of holiday radiance and clear dark skies filled with hundreds of twinkling stars.

He knelt to the ground on one knee and held out a tiny black velvet box. Opening it slowly, he looked up at Kate, who was smiling down at him with tears in her eyes.

"I love you so much. I have since the first time I heard you laugh. I loved you even more after the first time I saw you cry. I want to continue to bring you laughter and continue to wipe your tears for the rest of our lives. Will you do me the honor of marrying me?"

"Yes!" she yelled. "Yes!" Kate pulled John up from the ground. She gently grabbed his face with both hands and gave him a long passionate kiss that outwardly exuded the intense love between them.

It was the very first time I had ever witnessed a marriage proposal, and I captured it all on film. *I truly love my job.*

CHAPTER TWO

W eeks of counting down had ended. My older brother, Oliver, who just one month prior turned thirty-three, was finally here. Every time he came, I latched myself onto him as soon as he arrived and did not detach until he left again. It had been so difficult only seeing him in person twice a year for the past five years. Each year became a bit easier, but it still hadn't felt the same without him around all of the time.

My parents had five children, and Oliver was the oldest. He was three years older than Elijah, my other older brother. Two years later came Paityn, who's three years older than me. Ashton was the baby.

I was the only blonde in a family of brunettes, and Paityn was a clone of Mom, with brown eyes and brown hair, standing five feet tall and had a medium build. All of the boys had brown hair and blue eyes like Dad, and the four of them shared similar heights between five feet, eight inches and five feet, ten inches. My brothers got their athletic figures from my dad, but they were all involved in some sport or another over the years as well. I was lucky enough to reach an average height for a woman, five feet, five inches, and I was fairly slim, which always made me feel like I could eat as many carbs as I wanted. *I'm sure it won't be that way forever though.*

Oliver and I had gotten pretty close over the years. In middle school, he used to drive me to my soccer games and dance practices when my parents weren't available. When I reached the tenth grade, we started going to the gym together on occasion to do cardio or lift weights. We also used to go to the movies once a month and then spend the rest of the night quoting the flick and talking about which actors we liked best. Years later, we would go out to hear bands play. I would invite my girlfriends, and he'd invite all of his guy friends. We were all one big happy family.

One day, Oliver received a call about a nursing supervisor position at a well-known hospital in San Diego, California. He completed a phone interview, and then flew out to meet with a panel of board members and other supervisors at the hospital. He was offered the job the next day and promptly accepted. All of his hard work at his previous hospital in the nursing department had paid off, and he embraced the opportunity for a change. The reality had to be faced that Oliver was moving to the other side of the country.

We all vowed to go out and visit him in San Diego as soon as possible. A year after he moved to California, I booked a flight and set up an itinerary with Oliver for the week. We traveled all over the west coast, from Coronado Beach to Venice Beach. We saw the Hollywood sign and shopped on Rodeo Drive, and we even went to Disneyland in Anaheim. He told me all about his new position and about the team of people he worked with. He showed me his office and introduced me to some of his coworkers, who shared stories of their times together with him. Oliver seemed happy, really happy, and that made me happy. All of his dreams had come true, and the only thing missing in his life was someone to share it with.

Oliver was selective, and he always had been. He had certain qualities he looked for in women and rarely made exceptions. He also had a type he dated regarding physical features, favoring only women who were short with dark hair. The person Oliver would spend the rest of his life with had to be easy going. He needed them to have a sense of humor and share a lot of the same interests as him. Oliver had one girlfriend in high school, that he dated from the beginning of his junior year until right after graduation. The relationship ultimately ended because she was moving far away for college, and neither of them wanted to try the long distance thing. Since then, he dated several other women, but the relationships never lasted for one reason or another. Things never worked out, or maybe they did if you look at it in a "everything happens for a reason" kind of way. I believe things happened the way they were supposed to, and I had a good feeling that he was going to find his person in California.

This was Oliver's fifth year coming home for the holidays. The James' family time was too good to resist, and we would never let him anyway. We argued over who would pick him up from the airport and see him first. We would all go, but there would be no room in the car for luggage. Oliver always came home two days before Christmas and left two days after we celebrated the new year. I think some people would be overwhelmed with the schedule our family keeps at the holidays, but we enjoyed it; it was our tradition.

We hosted the Feast of the Seven Fishes at our house on Christmas Eve, which came from our mom's Italian heritage, and together attended mass at midnight. On Christmas Day, we gathered around the dining room table for breakfast before we exchanged gifts. We even wrapped presents for Harley, our yellow Labrador retriever. She turned eight this past year, and she had been opening presents since the first Christmas we had her as a puppy. She used to steal wrapped presents from under the tree that did not belong to her and rip into them with her teeth and claws until she would reveal the gift. Once she realized it wasn't edible, she would leave it and find something else to entertain her. It was only natural that we started wrapping a few for her each year to open, and she learned not to take anything we didn't give to her. Harley was intelligent, loving, and sweet; she was such a special dog.

Christmas dinner was celebrated with our grandparents on Daniel's very Irish side. Dad hated it when I called him Daniel, almost as much as Mom hated it when I referred to her as Isabel. I did it sometimes just to get a reaction. After dinner, we ate way too much dessert and played a variety of games. The day after Christmas, we headed over to my aunt's house for her annual holiday party. Isabel's sister invited nearly thirty people over for what felt like a giant cousin reunion. I wouldn't trade those three days of family fun for anything in the world.

This year, Dad went to the airport to pick up Oliver by himself. My brother, not usually one to overpack, asked us to send only one person because he'd brought extra luggage. I felt my blood pressure rising as my dad left to pick him up; I could not wait for them to return!

When Dad came home from the airport with Oliver, they did have some extra luggage - enough, it seemed, for *two* people.

"Hi! Why are you two carrying so many bags? Overdo it with your Christmas shopping this year?" I wanted to hug him, but his hands were completely full.

"Hey, Soph! It's so great to see you. Where are Mom and

Ashton? I have a surprise." Oliver placed the bags down by the stairs and I followed him, intrigued by the idea of a *surprise*.

"Mom is grocery shopping, and Ashton is still at work. They should both be home soon. Tell me! What is the surprise?"

"Chloe, it's okay to come in now," Oliver yelled out to someone in the driveway with a light in his eyes I had not seen in a very long time. He had a friend with him from California. Not just a friend, a girlfriend. It was *his* girlfriend.

CHAPTER THREE

Ashton was our younger brother. He was seventeen years old and a senior in high school. He worked part-time at the nearby coffee shop, but it had recently felt like he was never home. Mom thought he might be getting into trouble with a new crowd. Dad thought he might have a girlfriend and did not want to tell us. I thought he seemed slightly depressed. When the holidays were over, I planned on digging a bit more to gain some clarity on the situation.

Once Mom and Ashton were home, everyone sat around the kitchen table trying to catch up. We wanted to get to know Chloe, but we did not want to interrogate her. I had a hundred questions I wanted to ask. I decided to start with inquiring about how they met and how long they had been dating. It turned out they met back in the summer in Downtown San Diego at a concert and had their first date the following week. Chloe was nice, and she was really funny, and she had a quick wit that matched Oliver's perfectly. She was a mixture of Chinese and Japanese, had long brown hair and brown eyes, and was a tad shorter than him. Chloe worked as an early childhood school teacher out in San Diego, and she was close with her family as well. I liked her, and through conversation and observation of body language, I could see Oliver did too. He liked her *a lot*.

"Ashton, how is school going? Have you heard back from any colleges?" Oliver made an attempt to divert the attention.

"School is fine. Grades are average, maybe a little above. I have heard back from one college." Ashton replied to Oliver vaguely.

"Whoa, there, buddy! Don't share too much with us." We missed Oliver's satire around here.

"I don't know. I just want to graduate and be done with that place. I feel like I have been living in this bubble for years, where everyone knows everything about everyone. Nothing can ever stay private, and people are always passing judgment. I can't wait to go away."

It just hit me at this moment that Ashton was leaving. He should've been the last to go, but I had been too attached to the house and my family to move out. I even commuted to college because I couldn't bear the separation. My anxieties about living alone also prohibited me from getting my own place. I was going to be living all alone with Isabel and Dan, and Harley too of course.

"What college did you get into, Ash?" Oliver pushed for more information.

"An acceptance letter came in the mail last week for Belmont University in Tennessee. It's my first choice and far enough away from here. I'm committing after the holidays."

I searched Mom and Dad's faces for reactions. They already knew.

"Ashton, I don't think I realized you were going so far away. Are you sure you are ready for that?" I wondered if he really had thought this through.

"Soph, I have *been* ready. Riley is going too, so I will already know at least one person there."

Riley was Ashton's new friend from school. We had still yet to meet her, but he seemed to be her biggest fan. I suppose it helped knowing that he would have a friend moving to another state with him, and it was another place I would get to visit on occasion. I could check up on my little brother and add to my landscape photography portfolio while I was there. Every cloud had a silver lining.

Mom cleared the table and brought out the mouth-watering, irresistible chocolate lava cake dessert. *Why does she always do this to me? Damn that woman and her phenomenal cooking!*

Now that we had grilled Oliver and Ashton over dinner, I feared my turn was coming next.

"Dad, what time is everyone getting here tomorrow?" I tried to deflect.

"Well, Paityn and Bradley are planning on getting here around four o'clock with Liam, and Elijah will be arriving with Bethany right before our signature cocktail hour."

I loved when all of us were together. Our family was large, and it had become so spread out over the years. Paityn, who was the middle child, had married Bradley four years ago and moved to Atlanta, Georgia a few months later. Right after their first wedding anniversary, Liam was born. He was about to turn three years old, and he was the most adorable toddler I had ever seen. I know, I was just a little biased with him being my nephew, but he really was super cute. His eyes were bright blue, and his hair was mostly brown with some natural blonde highlights. Paityn combed his hair back so that it had a slick but spiky look, and she and Brad always dressed him in button down shirts and jeans. The kid would definitely be a heartbreaker when he gets older. Hopefully, by then, Liam would be more into socializing. He was very quiet and shy, and he did not seem to like it when anyone entered his personal space. Paityn was certain that he would grow out of it once he started going to daycare.

Elijah was the second oldest, born three years after Oliver. He dated Bethany for five years before getting engaged, and they were married six months after the proposal. It was a small wedding in the park, just a few miles from their home in Pipersville, a couple of years back. They tried for a while to have a baby, and when Bethany finally did get pregnant, she had a miscarriage, which led to many months of grief. Elijah shared with me at Thanksgiving that their biggest fear is having history repeat itself. The only advice I had to offer at the time was to remain positive and to trust the timing of his life.

"Soph, are you inviting Raelyn or Kendal over for the Seven Fishes dinner?" Dad loved when the girls were over because they always laughed at all of his jokes.

"I don't think so, Dad. Raelyn's family will be celebrating Christmas Eve with Kevin's family, and Kendal has dinner plans at her grandmother's house. It will just be me, and I am perfectly fine with not having to entertain anyone."

"No date, Soph?" Oliver just had to go there.

"Nope."

"Have you been seeing anyone recently?" Oliver poked again.

"Nothing serious. I have a lot going on with work. I don't have much time to meet new people or even go out too often. Did I tell you about the crazy team photo shoot I had last week?" I made a solid attempt to dodge.

"Do you put yourself out there? There are a ton of dating apps."

I knew Oliver meant well, and I knew all about the dating apps; that was how Rae met Kevin. I had not gotten around to trying any of them, and I was not sure I ever wanted to.

"I am thinking about signing up for one, Oli, but I'll probably wait until the new year to set up a profile. I just really want to enjoy the holidays with my family." I doubted I was giving Chloe the best first impression of myself, but I could not tell all of them the real reason I was not dating at the time. I could not tell anyone. *I can't do anything until I know he is definitely interested and not off limits.*

CHAPTER FOUR

Journal Entry

I 'm stoked for Oliver. Ever since he and his high school girlfriend broke up, he's had the toughest time finding someone that made him feel anything real. I knew him going out to California would make a difference. When he got that job, I knew. Chloe is legit too. She's caring and genuine, and I could see her fitting in with our family. I hope she's it. Oliver deserves this. Dear God, let this be his person.

And while I'm praying, maybe we could make sure I end up with my person soon?

I know twenty-five is still young, but I want to be in love. I want to know what it feels like to have someone who cares that much about me, in that way.

I want to know what a lot of things feel like. There are so many missing pieces to my puzzle. One day, I will be established as a photographer. One day, I will move out of my parents' house and get my own place. One day, I will get married to the love of my life. One day.

CHAPTER FIVE

I t was hard waking up the next morning. We had been up
until after midnight sharing stories, listening to music,
and making cookies. I vaguely remembered eating a few
cookies too. Maybe I ate more than a few. I could never turn
down chocolate chip cookies, especially when they were
homemade. Chloe learned more about our family that night
before and how Oliver grew up. She told us about her family
too and what it was like growing up with two brothers. We
found some similarities in sibling relationships, which led me
to point out how well I thought Chloe would fit in. Oliver
urged me to contain my excitement when she was using the
bathroom, but I couldn't help being optimistic about his new
relationship.

I had to go to work for a few hours right after breakfast. A
woman that Mom taught with hired me to do a family
photoshoot at a nearby covered bridge. I was grateful for the
work, even if it was on Christmas Eve. Holiday shoots were
great because everyone was dressed festively and in good
spirits, so it didn't take a lot of effort to coordinate position or
make the group smile. Although, even when the work was a

little difficult, I truly enjoyed my job. There was no other profession I would want to do, and I did not think any other profession would suit me better either.

I did a combination of family photography, event photography, and landscape photography, but I wanted to expand into fashion and glamour photography, as well as fine art photography. I knew my time was going to come, as I had been doing photography since I was in high school. At first, it was just class work and me taking pictures of people I knew, and then I would snap pictures of landscapes on all of my vacations. I studied Art History and Film Production in college. The dream was to spend my life as a famous photographer. For the last three years since I earned my degree, I had been working in multiple cities within Pennsylvania, and I had also been hired for jobs in New Jersey and New York. I was thankful for all of the work that came my way, especially when I had the chance to be behind the camera in a place I had never seen.

While I was at work, everyone else went to the mall to do some Christmas shopping. Luckily, I never waited until the last minute, so I finished shopping weeks ago. I was going to head home after my shoot to get things ready for the night. Paityn, Bradley, and Liam were going to stay in the basement, which had been made into a family entertainment room with two couches that unfolded into beds. They always took the basement when they stayed over because it was big enough to accommodate the three of them, and they usually visited for a few days at a time. Oliver and Chloe were staying in the guest room upstairs, and Elijah and Bethany would spend the night in the loft at the top of the stairs between two of the bedrooms.

I searched for Harley's leash. She needed a long walk before our guests checked in. It was best to have Harley feeling tuckered out when people came over; otherwise, she would get herself all riled up. She had definitely calmed down over the years, but she still had this energy that Labrador retrievers never seem to lose. It was hard to believe she was turning nine years old this spring, especially when she tried to take me for a walk instead of the other way around.

As we walked down the paved driveway out to the road, Harley pulled me in every direction, sniffing the ground and the bushes. Another animal must have been there, and she was not pleased. This was her property after all, and there were no trespassers allowed without her approval. Harley was growing agitated. She began to pull me toward a bush at the end of our path. She sniffed and barked, and her hair stood up. I was anxious now, and I commanded her to settle down.

"Harley, stop! Sit!" I remained firm. She pulled me more, until her head was inside the bush. Something was clearly in there, but I did not want her to eat it or worse, get hurt trying to. I pulled Harley back with all of my strength. She finally sat, breathing heavily. A small, gray and white, baby bunny hopped out of the bushes. Harley watched, whining, resisting my hold on her. "No, Harley! Leave it alone. Stay!"

We waited for the bunny to disappear before continuing our walk. We walked down the road in complete silence for a while, and I looked down at Harley, trying to make her aware of the anxiety she gave me. I flipped my bottom lip up to show her I was sad, and I gave her those puppy dog eyes that she had given me over a hundred times. She looked up at me and tried to give me her paw. I could tell she felt badly for her actions. Harley was a good dog and always wanted to please everyone. If she thought you were disappointed in her, she could not bear it.

She moved closer to me and tried to give me her paw again. She licked my hand that was holding her leash, and she whimpered while wagging her tail. I bent down and let her kiss my face all over, and I smothered her with kisses right back. That was my girl.

We got back to the house, just as Paityn and Bradley were pulling up with Liam. Thankfully, Harley was exhausted and did not have it in her to act up when she saw them. Hugs were given all around, and Dad came outside to help them with luggage. I just saw Liam at Thanksgiving, and he already looked bigger.

"Paityn, what in the world are you feeding him?" I was half joking.

"He is a good eater, and cooking is what I do best!" Paityn laughed and looked at Liam.

"He is a hungry boy!" Bradley joined in.

Paityn was also being very literal with her humor. Cooking really was what she did best. She was a chef, and she was a spectacular one. I used to taste test all of her food when she was in high school taking culinary classes. I stopped being such a willing participant though when I realized I was putting on weight.

"How is work going, Paityn?" I was often curious what new meals were on the menu at her restaurant. It had been a while since I visited Georgia, and she was always kind enough to replicate the popular items when she came here.

"Work is great! We just added two entrees and a dessert to our dinner specials." She sounded so excited. I was proud of my sister for chasing her dreams and becoming so successful. How she felt about cooking was how I felt about photography, and we both knew our passion since middle school, so we had many years to practice and craft our skills.

"Brad is settling us in downstairs. When should we expect Elijah and Bethany?" Paityn asked eagerly. She was as excited as I was to have the whole family together.

"They should be here within the next couple of hours. You have to meet Chloe though!" I rushed my sister into the den, where Oliver, Chloe, Ashton, and Mom were having a discussion about which games we were going to play later. Dad was in the kitchen preparing the fried calamari.

"Oli! It is so good to see you! Who is your pretty friend?" Paityn cut right to the chase.

"This is Chloe, my girlfriend." Oliver said without any hesitation. To the contrary, he demonstrated a noticeable pride in his relationship. Paityn smiled from ear to ear at the news. I realized in that moment how fortunate I was to be part of a family who supported each other the way we did.

CHAPTER SIX

E lijah and Bethany rang the doorbell just before six o'clock that evening. The entire James family greeted them at the door, and Oliver made his introductions. Everyone had taken a liking to Chloe. Oli definitely picked a good one. Additionally, it was her first ever Feast of the Seven Fishes, which made us all feel a little better about stealing her away from her own family for the holidays. Christmas Eve at our house was a big deal, and it was guaranteed to be entertaining.

Cocktail hour had a way of revealing secrets from the year, and this time was not any different. I just wished we could have done a better job of getting Ashton to confide in us. Throughout the evening and the weeks leading up, it was obvious that something was going on with him.

Elijah shared with us that he and Beth were using a fertility program now to try and get pregnant, and Chloe told us how she was previously married and divorced due to infidelity. Paityn gave us insight into Liam's new daycare facility and his teachers. I rambled on about my recent jobs all over the state, hoping to prevent any further dating inquiries.

Dinner conversation was interesting, yet comical, but it was what occurred after dinner that really intrigued me. While most of the family was gathered in the family room trying to choose which game to play, we heard a knock on the front door. Usually people would ring the doorbell, which made me think whoever was there was trying to be inconspicuous. I stood up and peered into the foyer. Ashton darted down the stairs from his bedroom at the top of the landing and opened the door. An average height young man with short, dirty blonde hair and a slim build just like Ashton stood waiting. He appeared to be the same age as Ashton too, and he had an innocence about him that you could see in his dark soulful eyes. My younger brother welcomed the boy with a handshake that had to have been rehearsed at least one hundred times and then took him into the kitchen. I followed closely behind them. *What was going on?*

"Ash, who is your friend? I asked nonchalantly.

"Where did you come from, Sophia?" He seemed annoyed with me.

"I heard a knock and wanted to see who was there. Is this a classmate of yours?' I poked even harder.

"Yes, we go to school together. Sophia, meet Riley. Riley, meet Sophia." Ashton answered me dismissively.

"Oh, you're Riley? Wow! Excuse my surprise. It is so nice to meet you!"

I conducted some small talk with Ashton and Riley for a few minutes, trying to get a grasp on their friendship, and then I left them alone. When I joined the rest of the family, I told them that a school friend was here to see Ashton. Mom rose up and went to say hello, but they had already gone into the garage. I assumed they were playing video games or possibly exchanging Christmas gifts, since they were such great friends. All of these months, I thought Riley was a girl Ashton liked and that maybe their new relationship was causing him to have changes in his mood, but I guess I was wrong.

In the family room, Liam was sitting next to the Christmas tree repeatedly pointing to the pile of presents with dinosaur wrapping paper that Mom told him was from the family. This was his way of asking to open gifts. We decided it was okay for him to open just one, which brought a huge smile to his cookie crumb covered face. Liam carefully chose which present he wanted to open. It was a three-foot-tall by two-foot-wide box, and he tore right into it.

"Cars!" Liam shouted. "It cars!" He was so excited to discover six vehicles of a mixed variety and a lined carpet road with street signs and lights. Liam had a small obsession with cars, and Mom and Dad added to his collection any chance they could. I loved seeing little kids react to their gifts on Christmas.

Liam's bedtime had come and gone, and he was fighting his exhaustion. Paityn and Brad took him downstairs to their room to get him to sleep, but not before letting him put milk and cookies out for Santa and carrots out for the reindeer. Oliver and Chloe retired to their room as well, and the rest of us planned out our Christmas morning breakfast, assigning the fruit filled pancakes to Paityn of course. Bethany also enjoys cooking, so she volunteered to help Mom with omelets and cinnamon buns. She knew all different kinds of gluten free recipes because Elijah found out he had celiac disease last year, and we were more than happy to make accommodations for him.

Harley was whining to go outside, and Dad agreed to take her this time. While they were on a walk, I filled Harley's stocking with all of her favorite treats and a brand new, medium sized, pink squeaky toy. She would be ecstatic in the morning, right along with Liam. I went up to bed, waiting for

Harley to return and jump in to snuggle. I slowly dozed off, anticipating the events of Christmas Day.

CHAPTER SEVEN

I woke up with slobber all over my face.

"Harley, stop!" This had become a daily routine for the two of us. "I'm up, I'm up. Stop, girl!" Harley retreated and rolled over onto her back. Even with the excitement of the day, I still wanted maybe ten more minutes in bed. I wrapped myself around Harley and squeezed her until she wriggled away and leapt to the floor. She was definitely more eager than I was to end our slumber. It was time to head downstairs, and I was so glad I did not have to get changed; we all wore our Christmas pajamas to breakfast.

As I made my descent to the kitchen, the sweet aroma of cinnamon and berries filled the air. Harley's nose led her straight to the oven, where she sat and begged with her tail wagging and mouth salivating. I joined Harley right next to Paityn, almost drooling myself.

"Yum! It smells delicious. Do you need anyone to test the product? We are happy to be at your service!" I offered as Harley tried to give Paityn both of her paws, in hopes of being rewarded.

Paityn bypassed me entirely and knelt down to pat Harley

on the head, "Girl, I will make you a little plate when it's time, but let's get something from your stocking to hold you over." To the stockings they went, and Paityn reached into the one embossed with the giant 'H' on its front.

"What did Santa bring you? I wonder!" Paityn enticed Harley and then pulled out a chewable pig ear. Harley sat and gave Paityn a high five, laid down, rolled over, and then gave a little bark to speak. "Good girl!" Paityn praised her. That would keep her plenty occupied until breakfast was ready.

Once the whole family was awake and in the kitchen, we sat down to eat the mouth-watering spread until everyone was completely stuffed and could not move, and it was not long before all of us gathered around the glorious Christmas tree. Liam was the only young child, so he opened his gifts first. Ashton went next, and then the rest of us followed. We saved our traditional sibling gift exchange for the end, since that was always the most fun. Each of us only bought for one person, a serious gift and humorous gift, which was sometimes a gag gift. We chose names from a bowl at Thanksgiving, and that was the person we were assigned to. It used to be just the five of us, but now we included Bethany and Bradley. If Oliver stayed with Chloe, she would surely be included next year, and I supposed eventually there would come a time when Ashton and I would have people to add to the group.

After all of the presents were distributed, unwrapped, and cleaned up after, Mom suddenly remembered there was one more.

"Sophia, go open the closet door in the foyer!" Mom sounded very mysterious.

"What is it, Mom?" I usually did not like surprises because I hated being caught off guard, but I did make exceptions for Christmas and for my birthday.

"I don't have any idea, honey. You should take it out of there and open it," she said with a thick tinge of mischief in her voice. I opened the door to find a tall, large box with a big red bow on it. *What could this be?*

"Mom, why did you hide it in here and not put it with the other gifts by the tree?" I pushed for more hints.

"It's not from me, Soph."

"Dad, did you get me another present?" My dad and I would sometimes pick up small trinkets for each other if we saw something that we thought the other would like, but this was a lot bigger than a trinket. Also, I did not see why he would do this for me and nobody else on Christmas.

"Sophia, it's not from me. Open it up, and find out." Dad urged me to get on with it, clearly growing impatient to find out what it was.

I carried the box into the living room, untied the bow, and cut into it with scissors we already had out for other packaging.

"Oh my!" I gasped with amazement. "A new tripod!"

"Who is this from?" I asked, surveying the room. Mom and Dad looked at each other puzzled, not seeming to have the answer I was looking for. "Paityn, Oli, Ash, Eli? Did one of you get this for me?" I searched their faces for clues, maybe the hint of a smile on their lips, or the shifting of glances from me to each other. Instead, there was nothing.

"No." They all said to me in near unison.

"It's not from any of us." Paityn affirmed and looked at the guys. They nodded in agreement.

I could not figure out where this had come from. There was no signature on the card, just a message that said, "Broaden your horizons." My mind wandered. I shifted my attention back to my parents, who *must've known* something.

I grinned at my mom, thinking I'd caught her in a fib. "Mom, you knew it was in the closet, so how did it get there?" Even if she hadn't been the one to buy it, she must have known who delivered it and was just keeping me in suspense.

"Sophia, it arrived just yesterday on the front porch with no return address label. I thought it would be fun to hide it since the sender was anonymous." While Mom explained her antics, the rest of the family looked baffled.

"Well, I am truly stumped. I cannot imagine who knows me well enough to think I would need a new tripod." I said to my whole family.

"Soph, maybe one of your girlfriends wanted to spoil you or a photography friend that you have done some work with was feeling generous?" Paityn tried to help me figure it out. "I suppose it could be something like that. I do have nice friends." I thought about the people who were closest to me and which of them would actually know to get such a gift. Then it hit me. *Maybe he would have. It's not out of the realm of possibility, since we have spent time together in the field and are very close.*

I put the tripod in my bedroom and got ready for mass. The rest of the family put on their holiday best, and we took two cars over to the church. Luckily, Paityn drove an SUV, as well as Mom, so there was plenty of room for all of us between the two vehicles.

When we entered the bright, elegant church and chose our seats toward the back row of pews, I saw the Taylors, otherwise known as Raelyn's family. Her parents lived a few minutes away from us, and her brother rented a condo in a small development at the end of their long road, so we were all members of the same parish. They quickly approached and scurried into the pew behind us.

"Hey, Rae! Hey, Kev! Hello, Mr. and Mrs. Taylor, and Owen!" I whispered to them enthusiastically.

She had such a great family, and they always made me feel like a part of it. Her older brother, Owen, was the best they came. He was funny, interesting, kind, and smart. He even studied photography in college, just like me, commuting to a nearby university instead of living away. Neither Rae nor Owen wanted anything to do with living in the dorms, which was another thing we had in common. The three of us also enjoyed doing many of the same activities, so it was very easy to hang out randomly over the years.

Throughout the service, I still had the gift on my mind, and I continued to wander to thoughts of who could have sent me such a thoughtful and surprising gift. I had an inkling of who was behind it, but I couldn't be certain. I needed confirmation. When the last song was coming to an end, our family and the Taylors walked out to the crowded parking lot together. We said our loving goodbyes, and when Owen hugged me, he asked me if I had received anything special for Christmas. Upon waiting for a response, he displayed this devious but adorable smirk on his face. *I knew it.*

"It was *you?*" I asked him, trying to appear surprised.

"I thought you could use an upgrade, based on the last shoot we teamed up on," he sweetly replied. "Do you like it?"

I was overcome with gratitude and almost couldn't find the words to express it.

"I love it, Owen! I cannot believe you did that. I don't even know how to thank you."

"Just use it often, and that will be all the thanks I need. We'll talk soon." He kissed me on the cheek before walking away, and our families wished each other a great holiday.

Later at dinner, Grandma and Grandpa on Mom's side told us stories about their most recent cruise to the Caribbean and got themselves acquainted with Chloe through a series of invasive and overly-interested questions. But she handled them like a champ, a true indication of what a stellar match she made for Oliver. Elijah and Bethany shared the news that they were trying to conceive through more modern methods, and Ashton told them all about moving to Tennessee for college. Liam had been such a good boy all day, that I knew it was only a matter of time before he had one of his low-key temper tantrums. We almost made it through the last course of dinner, when he started tossing random items from the table onto the floor, along with the toy car Bradley insisted he have by his plate. As a result, Paityn then had to excuse herself and calm him down in their room in the basement. She managed to get him to fall soundly asleep after only a half an hour, which fortunately meant that he was down for the count, since it was already after seven that evening.

When she returned, Grandma inquired about his speech and vocabulary, as well as his tendencies to attach himself to both Paityn and Brad. Grandma rarely beat around the bush, and Mom told us she had always been that way, which is why she had a better relationship with Grandpa growing up. Luckily, they seemed to be used to that particular line of questioning and responded accordingly.

"Grandma, Liam is just quiet. He gets very shy and feels most comfortable around Brad and myself." Paityn tried to explain, but I didn't think she believed everything she was saying. There was more to it. My take was that she and Brad were in a bit of denial about Liam's development, but I was not a doctor. Grandma wasn't either, but that didn't stop her from voicing her opinions.

"I don't know darling. I think you might want to get him evaluated over the next few months. He should be much more verbal. I'm just saying is all," Grandma offered as Paityn went on to explain how he goes to regular check-ups with the pediatrician and that they are staying on top of it.

"Who wants dessert?" Mom interjected, which was a very delightful distraction. The assortment of pastries, pie, and chocolate pudding was too much to resist. Everyone filled up on sweets and migrated to the family room to further admire the astonishing lights on the Christmas tree and relax after a very lovely but exhausting day.

I went up to my bedroom to change into pajamas and checked my phone before heading back downstairs to rejoin the festivities. One new text message appeared on the screen: *It was great to see you today. I really hope you enjoy the tripod. Merry Christmas! - Owen*

CHAPTER EIGHT

Journal Entry

I planned on enjoying the tripod. I was already enjoying the tripod, just looking at it. This is not just equipment; this is a symbol. It signifies a shift. I think I actually might have a shot, and I don't just mean with the improvement of my photo shoots.

He's telling me there's a chance. He's saying he's interested. Six years later, and it's finally my time. I think so anyway. What else could it mean? Friends don't just buy you gifts like that, not such meaningful ones, and they don't usually give them to you in a surprising and mysterious manner the way he did. He's ready, or almost ready, to make some moves, and I need to be ready too. How have I kept my feelings for Owen hidden so long, from him and from his sister, my best friend? Have I really been so hell bent on denying the truth to everyone and convincing myself that it would never happen? I think that's why I've been so good at it. I believed it myself that it would never come to fruition for various reasons. The game *has changed now though. I'm off the bench. I have to get my head in it and work on how I will approach this moving forward. God, help me!*

CHAPTER NINE

"Sophia! Wake up!" An incessant knock on my bedroom door and Dad's voice urging me to get out of bed stirred me from my restful sleep. I glanced at my phone to see it was almost ten o'clock in the morning. I could not believe I had slept this late.

"Give me a minute," I shouted back at him through the door. *Where's Harley?* I lifted the comforter to see if she was curled up in her most favorite position by the foot of the bed, but there was no sign of her. I bent down to take a peek underneath the bed frame. *Where is that dog?* I anxiously rushed to get dressed and aggressively swung my bedroom door open.

"Dad! Have you seen Harley?"

Dad was standing at the top of the landing in the loft, where Elijah and Bethany had spent the night.

Ignoring my question, he handed me a navy blue and white duffle bag. "Soph, can you take this downstairs with you and leave it by the front door?" He turned back to them to continue helping them get the space back in order.

I was sad to see them go, but they usually made an

appearance at the annual holiday party held by our aunt and uncle, which just so happened to be that night. I took the bag down and left it in the foyer on the carpet by the front door, still searching for Harley as I ventured through to the kitchen.

The James' house had a fairly open concept throughout its lower level, where each room flowed into the next, with the exception of the powder room. Mom had used her wonderful interior design skills to turn that into a beach-themed escape. The other rooms downstairs possessed a country, rustic feel and a contemporary atmosphere simultaneously.

I called for Harley, knowing my voice would carry, but she did not come. Then I realized nobody was around. *Where is everybody?* I waited for Dad, Elijah, and Bethany to transport their luggage into Elijah's truck and then asked again. Only this time, I wanted to know where everyone was and why I was not invited.

"Soph, you were sleeping in, which you never do, so we did not want to bother you." Dad tried to explain.

"Where did they go, and how long ago did they leave?" I wondered if I had time to pull myself together and join them.

"Paityn and Bradley thought it would be nice to take Liam over to the park by the elementary school since they have a pond and a playground." The weather *was* unusually warm for late December. We always hoped for snow that time of the year, but the temperatures had been in the sixties the last three days. Even Chloe was counting on a white Christmas since she had never had one living in California. "Oliver wanted to show Chloe more of the town, and Mom decided to bring Harley. They left about thirty minutes ago. Once Elijah and Bethany leave, we can meet up with them, if you want."

After doling out a quick goodbye, with their assurance I would see them later at night, I ran upstairs and hopped in the shower, sprayed my hair with some curl-boosting, frizz-fighting product I had just ordered online that guaranteed beach waves all year round, added some lotion and deodorant, and got dressed. I figured I could add some mascara and lip gloss in the car. Dad had the car running when I reached the porch, and we made it over there in record time.

When we closed the doors of the red Jeep, we scanned the park. I spotted them over by the picnic tables, but I noticed something as I was walking toward the family. *Where is Ashton?*

"Mom, is Ashton here too?" I continued to look around the area as I was waiting for a response.

"He said he was going to get coffee with Riley." Mom told me with a smile on her face. "I really hope he will give us the chance to meet her soon. I was expecting to over the holidays, but I suppose he's not ready."

I decided at that moment that it was not my place to give them any information about Riley. That was Ashton's business. Although, I could not help wondering why we had all assumed Riley was a girl. It was a unisex name after all. *Had Ashton led us to believe that she was? If so, why would he do that?* I had no explanation of his most recent behavior.

"Maybe we can see if Ashton wants to bring Riley to the party tonight?" I posed the question carefully.

"Yes, that is a great idea! I will send Ashton a text message suggesting he do just that." Mom took her cell phone out of her purse. It was always humorous watching her text.

I sat next to Chloe and Oliver on the other side of the picnic bench and observed Liam playing with Paityn and Bradley near the pond.

"Duck!" Liam exclaimed.

"Yes, that is a duck, Liam," Bradley praised him. "Do you want to feed the duck? I will get some crackers from the table."

"Duck cwacker, Daddy!" Liam was very pleased with the idea. He waited patiently while Bradley scooped up the crackers and brought them back to where Paityn and he were sitting a few feet from the water.

"Here you go, bud! Let Mommy help you. Be careful."

I sat at the table with a clear look of wonder on my face.

"Hey, Soph, what's wrong?" Oliver noticed how deep in thought I was.

"Well, I am just a little bit worried. Chloe, you work with very young children, correct?" It occurred to me that she may have had some insight that I did not.

"Yes, I teach pre-school. Why do you ask?"

"The more time I spend with Liam, the more I think something is off. His dialogue and vocabulary are delayed, and the manner in which he socially engages with the rest of the family seems a little more than introverted. I am not around children that often, but I do remember Ashton being that age, as well as some of our cousins. Paityn thinks daycare will help him because he will be around a lot of other children his own age and will therefore learn from them and mimic behaviors and skills. I'm not sure she is right."

"I have to admit, Liam does appear to be somewhat developmentally delayed, based on my work experience and some babysitting experience. However, some toddlers don't speak much at all until they turn three or a few months after, and then they don't stop talking. It may be too early to tell. He also could just be really attached to his parents because he is with them more than anyone else and hasn't started schooling yet." Chloe gave me some comforting feedback.

"You could be right, Chloe. Mom, what do you think? You are a special education teacher. Do you think Liam will progress to the appropriate level as he gets older, or do you think it is possible that he has a disability that has not been diagnosed?" I realized I put Mom on the spot, but she did work with that specific population.

"Honey, I would be lying if I said I did not have my

concerns about Liam. Some of his behaviors are alarming, but he is happy and healthy, and he began crawling and walking when he was supposed to. He even started dancing to music as soon as he was able to stand on his own. If the worst thing is that he has a language issue or that he might fall somewhere on the autism spectrum, then we should count our lucky stars. It could be much worse." Mom put my mind at ease for the time being.

They were both right. It probably was too soon to make any clear diagnosis, and Liam was a happy kid. He did great at his check-ups with his pediatrician, who Paityn trusts would be making recommendations for evaluations if he believed it was time.

"Ashton texted back. He said he cannot bring Riley to the party tonight because he already has plans with his own family. Ashton says maybe we will meet Riley another time soon." Mom robotically read the text message, which made me laugh and soothed my disappointment that the family would have to wait longer to find out who Riley was.

When Dad came over from playing fetch with a lethargic Harley, we ventured back home to the house. My phone started ringing as I was walking through the front door into the foyer.

"Hey, Rae! What's going on? How was the rest of your Christmas?" I could not wait to hear details.

"It was great, Soph! Thanks for asking. Kevin and I had both of our families over for dinner, so I cooked. It turned out better than I expected. I hope yours went well. Owen says hi!"

"Hi, Owen!" I hoped he got my text back last night, thanking him again for the gift. "What are the two of you up to?" I tried not to sound too curious.

"Kev had to go to work today, so I stopped over at the magazine to get some things done myself. While here, I ran into Owen picking up a paycheck from his last assignment. We were just talking about going out tomorrow night for dinner and drinks. Would you want to join us? It will be me and Kev, and Owen of course. We can all catch up!" Raelyn made me an offer I could not refuse.

"Sure! I'll be there! Text me with the location and time, and I will see all of you then." I accepted with more excitement than I wanted to let on. *I hope Rae didn't notice.*

After we hung up, I ate lunch with everyone and then excused myself from the dining room table, saying that I had to go pick out an ensemble for the party later on.

Truth be told, I just wanted to go admire the tripod again.

CHAPTER TEN

A unt Capri and Uncle Alex lived in the city, about a forty-five-minute drive from our house. Oliver and Chloe rode with Paityn, Bradley, and Liam, which meant Ashton was coming with me, Mom, and Dad. This provided me with the perfect opportunity to try to inquire more about Riley, hoping that Ashton would clarify gender for our parents.

"Ash, how was coffee this morning?" I eased into the conversation lightly.

"It was good. We went to my work, since I can drink an unlimited amount of coffee at no cost," Ashton replied.

"When you say *we,* you mean you and Riley?" I tried to be subtle.

"Yes, Soph, I was with Riley. Why?"

"I'm just checking. I thought that's what Mom told me. It's a shame Riley had plans tonight." I still was not saying *he* because I wanted Ashton to say it.

Then, Ashton surprised me.

"Riley wanted to come to the party, but he promised his parents he would do a family game night with other relatives."

"He?" My mom hastily interjected.

I stayed quiet. *Take it away, Ashton.*

Ashton's face was expressionless.

"He, yes, Riley. Riley is my pal from school, the one I told you about. He's the friend who is going to the same college as I am." Ashton answered Mom with this nonchalant, casual explanation, acting as if she would have no reason to believe that Riley was not a guy.

"I do not know why, honey, but I thought Riley was a girl, a girl you were maybe dating or hoping to date. Is that not what you told all of us?" Mom shot Dad a glance for reassurance.

I knew I was not the only one who was under the impression that Riley was a girl Ashton was interested in. *Did he tell us that? Why did we all have that assumption?*

"No. I never said Riley was a girl. I'm not dating anyone. Riley and I have class together, and we became good friends."

Maybe he did not tell us he had a girlfriend. Maybe we just wanted to believe that he was dating someone because that would give us a reason for his peculiar behavior over these last few months, or maybe it was the endearing way he spoke about him that made us all think he was female or an object of his affection.

"I will call Riley tomorrow and invite him over for New Year's Eve so everyone can meet him. Does that sound good?" Ashton tried to make all of us see that he was not hiding anything and had not lied to us when their relationship first began.

"Great! Tell him that the entire James family requests his presence. It is time we meet the young man that has been stealing all of your time, buddy," Dad said in jest.

Aunt Capri welcomed us to the party wearing a knitted red sweater and green jeans, with a string of holiday lights worn around her neck and snowman earrings hanging from her lobes. She was as festive as the elves at the North Pole, and her whole house from top to bottom looked like it had been decorated by one.

I spotted Elijah and Bethany in the kitchen with my cousin, Ryan, so I made my way through the small crowd, saying hello to other family members briefly on the way there.

"Long time, no see!" I said to Eli and Beth, and then I greeted my cousin with a hug and a kiss on the cheek.

"Sophia, I was just asking your brother if you are seeing anyone. I brought a coworker with me tonight, and I think he would be perfect for you. I was hoping to introduce the two of you, if that's okay. Elijah here says you don't have a boyfriend right now. Is that true?" Ryan asked.

"That is true. I do not have a boyfriend. I'm not the biggest fan of being set up though. It always makes me nervous, and I feel all of this pressure to hit it off. I would rather not." I kindly declined Ryan's offer.

"Relax, Soph! There is no pressure to hit it off. I just thought you could meet him and see if you two have anything in common. He's a good person and a reliable guy." Ryan persuaded me to be open-minded. *I don't want to get to know another guy right now. Owen is the only one on my mind.*

"Alright, I will say hi, but give me a few minutes. I want to try one of the gingerbread martini's Uncle Alex is making." I figured one drink might help take the edge off.

Half an hour later, while I was in the basement with some of my other cousins, getting a stick ready to play pool, Ryan approached me. With him was a guy about six foot two with slicked back dark hair, wearing a long-sleeved, button-down shirt with jeans and brown shoes. He had blue eyes and a great smile. *So far so good.*

"Sophia, this is Marcelo, but everyone calls him Marc. He works with me at my accounting firm. Marc, this is my cousin, Sophia. She is a photographer in Bucks County. Do either of you need a drink? I am grabbing one." Ryan did the introduction and made an obvious excuse to leave.

"I will take another gingerbread martini," I said.

"I'm on it. I will get you another beer, Marc. Be back soon."

Ryan went back upstairs, and I asked Marcelo to be my partner for the next game of pool. This way, we could play and talk at the same time. He was courteous and very well-spoken, and he had just recently accepted a position at the firm with my cousin. He asked me all about my interest in photography and what made me go into the field. We actually got along pretty well.

Ryan returned with our drinks and chatted with us for a bit, and then he subtly disappeared again. I was enjoying the engaging conversation with Marcelo, who really did seem like a good guy. *Why was he single?*

As the night moved forward, we talked about the towns where we'd lived and where we went to college. He told me how he had never been married or engaged but how he had been in two serious long-term relationships. He ended the last one almost two years ago, and he had not yet met anyone else that was worth trying to build a life with. Marcelo then asked me why I was single and if I had ever been married or close to it. I started with the truth, that I had not ever been married, nor had I been engaged. Next, I did what I always do when someone asks me about my dating life. I lied.

"I guess my work keeps me so busy that I haven't ended up in anything serious lately."

"Could it be that maybe you are just not letting anyone get close to you out of fear of getting hurt?" Marcelo's effort at providing insight was remarkable, and he was half right. I haven't been letting any guy get close to me, but it was not because I was afraid to get hurt.

"I don't know exactly. You might be onto something." I told him what I thought he wanted to hear.

"Do you want to give me your number? I'd love to hang out with you sometime. If nothing else, we could form a decent friendship."

"Sure. Give me your phone, and I'll put it in," I said with a smile.

Marcelo has my number now, but I doubt I will be hanging with him again, unless we are in a group setting like this one. It has nothing to do with him though.

———

"Harley, what an interesting night! Do not pull, girl." She looked back at me as if to tell me I was walking too slow. "You do realize you woke me up at seven o'clock to take you on your morning walk, and we did not go up to bed until after midnight?" There was no answer. Harley was a great listener, but a strong conversationalist, she was not.

I told her everything, and this time was no different. I shared with Harley the events of the night before and the events to come that evening. She wagged her tail swiftly whenever she heard excitement in my voice.

"Are you ready to head back? We have to say goodbye to Paityn, Bradley, and Liam soon." She grumbled a little and then allowed me to turn her around. This girl would have had me outside for hours at a time if she could.

We got home just in time to see Paityn and Brad packing Liam into his car seat. Just a few minutes later, I would have missed them altogether.

"I will miss you so much, Liam! Give Aunt Sophia a hug and a kiss!" I leaned down into the back of the SUV.

"Muh, So!" Liam said back to me, trying to imitate a kissing sound that he must have heard from his mom or dad and pronouncing my name the way he always did, without the rest of the letters.

"Have a safe ride back to Atlanta! Call me when you get there." I tried not to cry, but I couldn't keep my eyes from filling up as they pulled away. I would not see them again until the springtime when we would celebrate the Easter holiday.

Then there were six of us, well, seven if you count Harley, which we always did. We still had a few more days with Oli and Chloe, thankfully. *I wonder what they are up to tonight.*

"Siri, call Raelyn." The phone rang twice before I heard her bubbly voice.

"Rae, do you think that it would be cool if I invited Oliver and his girlfriend, Chloe, to come out with us tonight? They leave to go back to California in less than a week, and I want to hang with them as much as possible."

"That sounds great! I haven't seen Oli at all this trip, and I surely would love to meet Chloe. Bring them!"

"Awesome! Is Owen still going out too?"

"Yes! Owen actually got really cheerful when I told him you were coming. I guess he misses you."

"He probably misses my clever banter," I said to her with an effort to cover. I couldn't let her think I was into him. *Not yet!*

I found Oliver checking movie times in the den on the computer, so my timing was perfect. They were on board!

Fortunately, Rae sent me the name and address of the place we were going to, so I could dress accordingly. I slipped on a pair of tight blue high rise jeans and my leather cowgirl boots, and then I added a low-cut tank with a yellow and blue plaid shirt unbuttoned to complete the look. Oli and Chloe did not have boots to wear, but he put on a pair of jeans with a plaid shirt, and she also wore jeans but with a lacy top. We were set to go to Montana West.

We saw Raelyn and Kevin sitting at a table in the back behind the dance floor when we walked in. *Where is Owen? Did he not come?* A sudden feeling of disappointment flushed over my whole body. Rae would have said something if he bailed. At least, I thought she would. Maybe she didn't think it was a big deal if he wasn't there.

I felt a tap on my left shoulder, and before I could turn around, an arm wearing a sporty tan and black watch wrapped around me to hand me a beer.

"Owen!" I screamed over the loud music and the crowd. "Hey! Thank you so much for the drink. How are you?" I was so happy to see him. *Be cool.*

"Better now that you are here, Soph!" He flashed a smile that almost made me blush.

The four of us walked over to sit with Rae and Kev, and I quickly noticed there was a mechanical bull on the right side of the bar. I had never tried it before, but I'd always wanted to. *If I could get one of the others to do it, I was all for it.*

"Sophia, are you thinking of riding that bull? I see you staring at it!" Oliver asked me.

"I will if you will!" I shot back at him.

"Deal! Let's have more of these beforehand though, to lessen the pain of falling off." He pointed at my beer and then waved the waitress over.

We ordered more drinks and some food and caught up on life. Oliver told everyone the story of how he met Chloe, and I did not even mind hearing it again. Raelyn and Kevin shared hilarious marital moments, and Owen highlighted some of his recent work. He really was an excellent photographer, and I knew I could benefit from some extra field experience with him.

"Owen, you are also a full-time photographer, like my

sister here?" Oliver had not spent much time with Owen in the past.

"I am, that's right. It rarely feels like work though, when you love what you do." Owen answered in quote form, and then he turned the focus back to me. "Would you not agree, Sophia?'

"Absolutely! I could not see myself doing anything else. I would wake up at three o'clock in the morning to try to get the best light, and I have." I looked over at Owen.

"Cheers to that!" Owen raised his glass and softly clanged it into mine.

"Rae, did Soph tell you she met a guy last night?" Oliver asked as soon as the table was quiet.

I jerked my head in his direction, my eyes wide. "What? Oliver, stop! It was nothing. My cousin introduced me to his coworker at our aunt and uncle's holiday party. We chatted for a bit. It was no big deal."

"Sophia, you met a guy? Do tell!" Raelyn always had to have the scoop.

"No, it really was nothing at all. I was just being polite."

I noticed Owen's delightful facial expression deflate. *Dammit, Oliver.*

"I think we should all go dance!" I worked to change the subject quickly. "Anyone? Rae? Chloe? Owen?"

Owen's smile reappeared, and he stood to join me. Rae and Chloe then dragged Kevin and Oliver out to the dance floor too. I tried to dance with Owen in a way that looked friendly and not flirty, but I was not too sure I was pulling it off well. I decided next to pull out some of my best cowgirl dance moves and do some very fancy footwork with my boots. Owen grabbed my hand and twirled me around, bringing me back against him. I enjoyed it for a second, feeling the heat throughout my body, and then danced away to the girls and my brother, who were basically standing next to Kevin, doing the repeated step-together and bobbing their heads to the music.

"Show me what else you have!" Owen yelled over to me and held out his hand again. He was really feeling the beat. I then jokingly did a little hoe-down back to him, and he twirled me around again, this time not letting go of my hand. I shot him a look that told him to be careful. We were not alone there.

"I'm going to use the restroom and grab another drink. Anyone need a refill?" I offered before leaving the group.

"I need one!" Rae exclaimed. "Light beer, bottle!"

"I'm ready for another too. I'll come to the bar with you." Owen was not doing a good job of being subtle. *Why was he being so lackadaisical?*

I used the restroom and then met Owen over at the bar. He was ordering a round for everyone, and I slipped up next to him to scare him like he did to me earlier in the night when we first walked in.

"Hey, there! Is this stool taken?" I disguised my voice and threw some humor his way.

"Sorry, I'm waiting for my girl. She will be back any minute, so you had better get out of here." Owen dished it right back.

I sat down close to him, but not too close.

"So, while we have a minute, tell me how much you have been thinking about me." Owen had this perfect way of knowing exactly what to say to make me smile.

"I think about you all day, Owen. You are my first thought when I wake up in the morning and my last thought before I go to sleep. I dream about you, baby, every single night. Can you handle that?"

"I bet you do, Soph. Tell me more. I can most definitely handle..." Owen started laughing before he finished his sentence. I started laughing too and then subconsciously leaned into his shoulder.

"You are so much fun, Owen. I could do this for hours."

"Maybe next time, we can hang out without our siblings?" Owen whispered in my ear. "What do you think?"

"Well, that sounds really great. Does that mean you are totally free now? I don't have to worry about your ex contacting me, do I?" I asked him.

I really was unsure of his current status, which is also one of the reasons I was nervous about carrying on with him publicly. The last thing I needed was for people to think I was trying to steal him from anyone. The other reason was that I didn't know how comfortable Raelyn would be with her best friend dating her brother. It never came up all of these years because when we all first met, I was dating a guy from college, and by the time I broke up with him, after almost two years, Owen had a girlfriend. He had that same girlfriend up until about a year ago, but the way Rae talked about her, something might still be there.

"Sophia, it's definitely over with Jade. Did you actually think I was still with her and showing interest in you at the same time?"

"I just didn't know what the story was; Rae kind of made it seem like things were complicated, so I took that as maybe something was still going on."

"We were talking here and there, and she even asked if we could patch things up at one point. I gave it serious consideration, but I knew we would continue to have the same problems we had for the full three years we were together. Nothing changes if nothing changes. We tried to stay friends, but it didn't work. I moved beyond it."

"Thank you for sharing all of that with me, Owen. I appreciate it. I'm glad to know I'm not stepping on any toes too if we do hang out."

"Definitely not! We do have one other small problem though, Soph. I have to speak with my sister about our deal."

"What deal do you mean?"

Just as I said the words, I felt someone tickle my back. Raelyn popped around to show her face. We sat there speechless.

"Busted!" She called us out.

"What? What do you mean?" I acted clueless.

"You two are over here helping yourselves to our drinks! You guys better not have done a shot without me!" She grabbed a beer off of the bar for her and one for Kev and told us to hurry up. Once she was out of earshot, we both started to laugh.

"Can I call you later?" Owen asked as we stood up.

"You better!" I said as I slid my right hand down his left arm, locked my fingers in his discreetly, and smiled. "Don't keep me waiting." *I am in so much trouble.*

CHAPTER ELEVEN

Journal Entry

Tonight was a good night. It was the best one I've had in a long time.

I could really see myself with Owen. He gets me like no other guy ever has. He sees me. He pays attention to what I say and what I do. When I'm with him, it feels right. But what if Rae doesn't think it's right? I don't know what I would do. It's not like I can just turn my emotions on and off. I can't just pretend I don't care. But I guess I'd have to try and get over it. Losing my friendship with her is not an option. Losing my friendship with him is not an option either.

Dear God, please help me to navigate all of this properly. My anxiety is through the roof just thinking about being honest with Rae and worrying about potentially missing an opportunity for real love.

I know if I want anything to change in my life though, I have to start taking initiative and making moves, rather than just wishing for things to come.

CHAPTER TWELVE

The rest of the week went by in a blink. Before we knew it, we were waking up to a whole new year and spending our last couple of days with Oliver and Chloe. It was heartbreaking to drop them off at the airport, but at least I was the one to take them. Mom and Dad fought me on it, but I refused to give in.

At home, things were strangely quiet. Ashton was either at school, work, or with Riley, when he was not hiding in his room. Even when Riley came over for New Year's Eve, we barely saw the two of them, but everyone said he made a decent impression on them. Mom went back to teaching right after the holiday break ended, and Dad held long hours at his engineering firm. Most days, it was just me and Harley, when I was not out on a shoot.

January was typically the absolute worst month for work in the photography business. On occasion, I would land a good job for a winter wonderland event or get hired to do a wedding for a couple who knew it was the most cost-effective time of the year to get married.

Luckily, I had a best friend who wrote for a local magazine

and was always in need of photographs showcasing nature in every season. I left early the next morning for the Poconos, where my job consisted of capturing the true essence of a popular ski resort called Appalachian Blue. I had to do a full spread of the mountain, including food, lodging, and snow sports.

As I was packing for the long weekend, a text from Owen popped up on my screen. He wanted to let me know that he was also hired by Raelyn's magazine to go to the ski resort, and he asked if I would want to drive there with him instead of taking two separate cars. At first, I was a little surprised to hear that two photographers would be working on the same assignment, but then I remembered that Raelyn had a habit of recommending both of us for jobs there. It did make sense to drive together, so I accepted his offer and asked him to pick me up.

Driving up to the Poconos with Owen was a favorable experience, and it was not our first long drive together, although maybe our first one alone together. I had traveled with him and Rae many times to shore points in the summer months, but the three of us would just play road games or sing obnoxiously to the variety of music playing on the radio. With her missing, the vibe was different; we had some serious conversation, mixed in with our usual poking of jokes at each other.

"So, any word from your new love interest, Soph?

"You will have to be more specific, Owen. There are so many, I lose track."

"Funny! I'm sure there are, but I'm speaking of the one from your aunt and uncle's holiday party."

"Oh, him, yes! We have been out a few times, and he wants me to meet his family this month. Can you believe it?"

"Stop it! Really? I didn't think you even liked him. That is what you said anyway."

"Owen, I'm kidding. I haven't spoken to him since that night. I'm not interested."

"You scared me there, Soph!"

"Oh yeah? What has you so worried?" I smiled over at him from my close position in the passenger seat.

"What? I'm not worried. I am cool, calm, and collected." He tried to cover by acting casual, but I could tell the thought of me dating someone made him jealous. I hoped the weekend would give us a chance to figure out our next move.

"I think we should do some snow activities while we are here too. It would be a shame not to," I said.

"I'm in! I have not done tubing or skiing in years," he responded.

When we checked into the resort and received our room keys, we realized we were not only on the same floor, but we were next door to each other. The magazine must have booked the rooms at the same time. At least, I knew where to find him.

We settled ourselves in and devised a plan of attack. Owen suggested we do some skiing and then spend the rest of the day snapping shots of people snowboarding. I thought it would be best to do work and then play, so we made a compromise. We would alternate days, starting with the first day being work then play and the second day being play then work. There were several activities for us to do at Appalachian Blue, and there were a couple that I wanted to repeat.

Owen and I suited up and went up to the snowboarding peak of the mountain where we set up our equipment.

"Have I mentioned how much I love my new tripod?"

"Nothing but the best for you." He winked at me and moved himself closer. "The view is better from over here."

The mountains were covered in a blanket of white, powdery snow, and the boarders glided down them with skill and precision that made me so envious not to possess myself. I had never even tried snowboarding, mostly because I was afraid to fall over and over again and end up with huge bruises all over my body. Even after spending a full hour watching and photographing, I remained firm in the idea that this was a sport I would leave to the experts.

We went back to my room to share our work and provide each other with some objective feedback. I told Owen we should do one more shoot of snowboarders before we left the resort, and he recommended doing it an hour before sunset to get a different lighting from today. *We work well together.*

"Owen, I think it's time for snow tubing!"

"You don't have to tell me twice. Let's go!"

We flew down the smooth mountain more times than I could count, screaming and laughing and sometimes holding onto each other's tubes. Owen was so adventurous that we moved to the lane with the most hills by the time we were finished. A feeling of elation came over me, as I thought about spending the rest of the weekend with someone so high on life. His attitude was truly contagious.

The resort had three main restaurants, which was quite perfect for our trip; we decided to try a different one each night, while snapping as many photos as possible of the meals. There was also a quaint little café to grab breakfast and lunch. That night, we chose Asian cuisine, which had hibachi too. I was pumped for both the demonstration and the food!

"You are supposed to catch it, Owen!" I laughed and mocked him, as he dropped every piece of chicken into his lap trying to maneuver the chopsticks between his fingers.

"It's not as easy as you make it look, sweetheart. I think I can do better if you feed it to me."

I took my fork and picked up a piece of teriyaki chicken from the plate in front of me and aimed it at his mouth.

"Here it comes, baby!" I tried so hard to do it with a serious face, but I could not help smiling.

"I think you should feed me more often," Owen said with a chuckle.

"What am I going to do with you?" I had said it rhetorically, but I honestly *did* want him to tell me what to do. *Why does everything have to be complicated?*

A roaring fire blazed below, and a crowd of guests gathered around it to roast marshmallows. That was something else that I had never quite gotten the hang of; I always somehow turned the marshmallow to charcoal. Nonetheless, a sudden craving for s'mores made my mouth water as the sweet scent of charred sugar mingled in the space. We paid our tab and leisurely strolled down the wooden staircase and out to the wide brick patio that was surrounded by newly planted evergreen trees. There were benches circled around the firepit, which allowed for many people to sit, though there were only a few spots left. Owen squeezed in smoothly next to an older couple and signaled with a come-hither motion of his hand for me to slide in beside him.

As we were sitting there listening to the fire crackle, close enough to touch but not quite touching each other, I thought about how much I did not want this weekend to end.

The next morning, I was awakened by light tapping sounds on the apparently paper thin wall behind my bed. It appeared to be a dream at first, and I, thinking I was at home talking to Harley, mumbled to the wall to be quiet because it was Saturday, and it was way too early to be rising.

The tapping sound grew louder and faster, and I finally realized that I was not dreaming and that I wasn't at home. The taps then moved from the wall to the door. I tied my bathrobe on and opened the door to see Owen standing there.

"Rise and shine, butterfly!"

"Ugh, Owen, what time is it?"

"It's about ten minutes after eight, and we have a busy day ahead. Get yourself ready and meet me down at the café. I will go and grab us a table and some coffee." He scurried away, and I hopped into a nice, hot shower, knowing I had only a few minutes to enjoy it. By some miracle, my hair still looked okay from last night, which saved me the trouble and time of having to wash, dry, and style it. I combed lightly through it, applied minimal makeup to my face, and pulled on my thermals, followed by snow pants, boots, and my enormous coat.

I grabbed my black camera bag, stuffed my wallet and cell in the front pocket, and then flew out the door. I jumped on the first elevator down to the café where Owen was waiting with extra large hot coffees at a table for two by the back window.

"Thanks, Owen. You are a lifesaver!"

"Anything for you, but I'll let you continue telling me how I am the best." He took a sip from his cup and grinned.

"Did anyone ever tell you your modesty is astounding?" I sipped and grinned right back at him, which was met with a warm chuckle.

"What do you think of skiing this morning and then spending the afternoon scoping out the rest of the property for landscape shots?" Owen asked.

Sounds perfect, but we should also get a few pictures of other skiers in their gear, and remember we have to take more snowboarding photos. We would have to do that at night about an hour before sunset."

"Yes, that is on the agenda, for sure. We certainly cannot do it tomorrow before we go home, with you being afraid to drive in the dark." Owen laughed at his own joke.

"It's not that I am afraid of the dark everywhere. I just

worry about the mountain deer and the unfamiliar roads that aren't well lit."

"I'm just messing with you, Soph! It is much safer to leave the resort before it gets late."

"Okay then, let's get to the ski lift before we have to waste the day away waiting in a long line" A sense of urgency started flowing through me.

Of course, when we got to the highest peak of the mountain, Owen rocked our ski lift chair back and forth a bunch of times. I swear, he loved to see me panic. I put up with his antics until we reached the top to get off, and then I pushed him out onto the snow.

It had been a few years since I'd been skiing, but the mechanics came back to me instinctually, and I was swept up in how invigorating the feel of the icy wind on my cheeks could be as I raced down the hill. Soaring down the steep mountain sent an adrenaline rush through me like nothing else and a powerful sense of freedom along with it. The experts say you are supposed to turn your skis in toward each other to create the shape of a slice of pizza if you want to slow down or stop. That never ever seemed to work for me, so I would simply throw myself to the ground when I got to the bottom of the hill. Though it was tricky to get back up, I usually found a way and hopped right back on the next available ski lift chair.

We were spent after almost three hours on the slopes, and we decided it was a good time to stop and grab our cameras out of the locker we were using by the main lobby. Photographing others skiing was not nearly as fun as doing it ourselves, but we snapped some incredible pictures, which rounded out the day to be enjoyable *and* productive.

We ate a late lunch at the same little café where we had

breakfast that morning, and then we roamed around the resort to see what else we could capture on film. By the time we made it back to the snowboarding area for round two, I was feeling the brisk cold chill of the mountain air settle deeper into my bones. I needed to get back to the room for my second shower of the day, only this one would be much longer in an effort to fully thaw out. I could not wait to feel the soothing hot water on my skin.

Owen and I had made a reservation at the Italian restaurant that night, and I was more than ready for some savory chicken parmesan with linguine and a bottle of red vino. When the waitress came over to take our order and pour water into the tall glasses in the middle of our table, I predicted what Owen might order. It was not much of a challenge, as he had a soft spot for lasagna ever since I had known him.

The dim lighting and old Italian music playing in the background almost made this feel like a romantic date. Owen and I were sharing a bottle of their finest cabernet, and it seemed like the perfect time for us to have a conversation that did not involve work stories or flirty banter.

"Owen, we really need to talk about...well, us." I put my hand over his and looked into his eyes, hoping for him to tell me that he too wanted to take the next step.

"I agree, Sophia. I have been dancing around what has been rapidly evolving between us over this past year, and I think you know why I have. But it's time to face the truth and stop hiding."

If he only knew that it had not just been a year.

"I think that maybe you are nervous of what your sister will think, the same way I am, of her best friend being with her brother." I stopped and waited for his response.

"There's that, but I also fear that you and I will lose our close friendship if things don't work out. If that happens, Rae could resent one or both of us because she might feel compelled to take sides or feel like she is stuck in the middle. Us taking a chance together could damage the relationships all of us have with each other, and I'd be lying if I said I wasn't scared."

"Owen, I hear what you're saying, and your points are valid. However, the alternatives are to either dismiss what we have or continue to lie to everyone else about our feelings. Personally, I know that neither of those options will make me happy, especially not for the long-term. If you want a future with me, we need to decide on a plan of action."

The waitress came by to see if we needed anything else before bringing us the check, and Owen ordered a second bottle of cabernet, since we had already finished the first one.

"If we are considering telling my sister, along with the rest of my family and all of your family too, we have to make a pact that we will not let it destroy the bond we have. I have never been able to open up to anyone the way I can with you. I feel like I can trust you and count on you like no other friend I have had. If I lost you, I don't think I could bear it."

"I feel the same way about you, and I would be devastated to not have you in my life. I need to be honest with you though." I glanced away and then back into his beautiful blue eyes. "I have known for a while now that our connection is much stronger than a friendship, but I refused to let you know, in case you didn't feel it too."

"I have to say I'm surprised to hear that, and I wish you would have let me know sooner, Sophia."

"I figured if you had...felt it, I mean, that you would have acted on it or said something, but you never did. So, I thought I was alone in my interest." My stomach immediately formed several knots. " I assumed I was not your type."

"You might not believe this, but I have been attracted to you from the first time I saw you. I would have asked you out if we were both single at the same time and if Raelyn and I hadn't made that agreement when we were in high school." Owen looked at me as if he was expecting me to know what he was talking about.

"What 'agreement' do you mean?" I asked curiously.

"Rae never told you? When she started high school, I was a junior. We figured it was a possibility that we might become interested in each other's friends, so we implemented the rule: neither of us was allowed to date the friends of the other. We stuck to it and then carried that out all through college and beyond and never deviated from it." Owen paused and reached out for my hand across the table. "I never thought I would have a reason to break that rule, until now."

"Well, you and Rae are all grown up. She may even give us her blessing to explore our relationship. Don't you think we owe it to ourselves to find out?" I smiled at Owen reassuringly.

"I think you're right, Soph. We will come up with a plan."

After we left the restaurant, I was suddenly in the mood to be in my favorite cozy wool pajamas, relaxing and watching a movie. I extended an invite to Owen, and he graciously accepted, joking that he would only come if we are watching a horror flick. Since I was like a kindergartener when it came to fright, we selected a rom-com.

Halfway through the movie, Owen fell asleep. Since I did not have the heart to wake him, I gathered the blanket from the edge of the bed, pulled it to our shoulders, and snuggled up next to him for the night.

I could get used to this.

CHAPTER THIRTEEN

W hen Owen dropped me off at the house the next evening, I walked inside to notice that Mom and Dad were nowhere to be found. I called for them and Ashton, but no one answered. There was no sign of Harley either. *Where is everyone?*

I made my way to the kitchen to get some water, and that was when I saw the back patio light on. I unlatched the sliding glass door and pulled it open. Harley came rushing toward me, panting and wagging.

"What are you doing out here, girl?" I questioned her as if she was going to tell me the whole story.

Harley ran back over in the direction she came from, so I followed her. It was very dark outside, but I could see a figure perched on the lounge chair by our covered pool.

"Ashton, is that you?" As I made my way closer, I could see him looking up at me.

"Sophia, I just need some time alone right now," Ashton replied, as he put his head back in his hands.

"What is going on, Ash?" I was really hoping he would finally confide in me, but I also knew what it was like to need to be alone. "I am happy to give you some space, but how about we go back inside? It's freezing out here!"

Ashton got up and came into the house with me. I walked into the living room and told him to sit down next to me. He resisted, but I persuaded him by telling him that I would share a secret with him if he talked to me.

"Okay, so what's up? Why were you sitting out back in January at night by yourself?" I asked him.

"Something happened tonight, and I just needed to get out of the house for some air. I wasn't out there long," he responded.

"Where are Mom and Dad?"

"They went to the movies about an hour ago."

"Well, what happened tonight that has you so upset?" I asked.

"If I tell you, Soph, you cannot tell anyone. I feel so embarrassed, and I don't know how to process it yet."

"I will not tell a soul." I crossed my heart with my finger. "As I stated earlier, I am pretty good at keeping secrets. What is going on?" I put my hand on his arm for encouragement.

"Well, Riley was here earlier. We were in the basement playing video games."

"Okay, that sounds like a typical hangout for the two of you. What was different about tonight?"

"Soph, I can't figure out how to say this. It's too weird."

I could tell he wanted to tell me badly, to get it out, but it seemed like he was scared to say the words because he was afraid of my reaction.

"Just rip off the band-aid. What happened?" At this point, I was dying to know.

"I kissed him!" Ashton blurted out.

I looked at him without judgment and took him in. He no longer resembled the small boy who used to steal my diary and read it aloud to his friends on the phone. He was all grown up in a way I hadn't realized before.

"Okay, I see. That's definitely a new development. Do you know what made you want to do it? Have you ever thought about it before tonight?"

"I don't know. There was this moment between us, and then he was staring at me awkwardly, so I just leaned in. I guess it has occurred to me before, what it would be like."

"How did he react to the situation? What did he say?" I asked him casually, trying to show him that this wasn't as uncommon as he might think.

"He backed away and asked me what I was doing. I didn't know what to say. I froze at first, but then I told him that I thought he knew." Ashton stopped, took a deep breath, and then continued. "He asked me what I thought he knew, and I said...well, that I thought he knew I might have been into him."

"He didn't know though? Did you explain to him that you had been having certain thoughts or feelings?" I was trying to help him run through it step by step to provide clarity for both of us.

"I tried to explain the best I could. I became very anxious and afraid of what he was thinking. I'm worried he won't want to even be friends now."

"Ash, this does not have to ruin your friendship. He needs to accept who you are, and you need to accept that he may not be interested in guys or that he may not feel *that way* about you."

"He left right after we talked, and I haven't heard from him since. I think he might be upset with me. What should I do?" Ashton was now asking me for advice, for the first time, and as much as I hated to see him struggling, I was glad I could be there for him.

"Give him some time. Riley probably feels slightly

blindsided, and he is most likely also afraid that what happened just destroyed what you two have. Try reaching out to him tomorrow after you both have slept on it."

Ashton became quiet and slumped back on the couch. I could tell his wheels were spinning. I sat there with him, thinking of what else I could say. Suddenly, he sat up and looked at me.

"Do you think I'm weird?" Ashton asked.

"No, not at all. There is nothing wrong with being interested in the same gender. I am curious though; do you like girls too or just boys?" I had a feeling he might not even know the answer to this question.

"I guess I am still trying to figure that out. I have only ever kissed one girl before, and now I have kissed one boy, if you count tonight." It was clear Ashton was very confused.

I took his face in my hands and locked eyes with him. "Hey, love is love, and do not *ever* feel ashamed of who you are." I pulled him in for a hug.

We embraced briefly, and then he pulled away, curiosity in his stare.

"You said you had a secret too. What is it?"

Oh no! I had forgotten all about that. Damn!

"I'm sure you don't want to hear about my problems, Ashton, after everything you are dealing with right now."

"No, I do. I need the distraction. Tell me!" Ashton did need to take his mind off of things, and I knew it could help me to talk about it.

"My secret is also about a relationship, two of them actually." I delicately began my story. "It turns out that I have to have an important conversation with Raelyn, and soon, about her brother." *Was I really going to say this out loud finally?*

"You have to talk to Raelyn about Owen? How come?" Ashton asked me with a bewildered disposition.

"Well, you know how you have been hiding your feelings for Riley?"

"Yeah…"

"I have also been hiding feelings."

"I don't get it, Soph. You can't have feelings for Raelyn. She's married!" He stared at me, and I gave him a minute to work through it in his head. "Wait...you said you had to talk to her about Owen. You have feelings for Owen?!"

There it is.

"Yes. Yes, I have feelings for Owen, strong feelings, and Rae has no idea. Owen doesn't even know how long I have had these feelings."

"Does Owen have feelings for you?" Ashton asked.

"He does now, but I don't know exactly how long it has been for him. He only shared that there's been an attraction from the beginning."

"How long has it been for you, Soph?"

I let out a sigh of anxiety and folded my hands in my lap.

"I have only ever admitted this to myself, Ashton, but I have been in love with Owen since that first summer we all started hanging together."

"When was that, like five years ago?" He was trying to get a clear timeframe.

"Six years now. That sounds crazy when I say it out loud."

"Why have you not ever done anything about it, and how come Owen or Raelyn haven't known?"

"It's all very complicated. I guess I was afraid to damage my friendships with both of them and ruin the dynamic the three of us have created. Besides, I had a boyfriend when Owen and I met, and then he had a girlfriend for a while. I was also worried he would never think of me as anything other than his sister's friend."

Ashton was being appropriately mature for this

conversation, and talking about it was making me feel like a boulder was being lifted from my shoulder.

"I think you should just tell Raelyn you're into Owen. The worst that can happen is that she might say she doesn't love the idea of you two dating each other. I don't know her as well as you do, but she doesn't seem that unfair. Maybe she would have hated it in the beginning, but it's been six years. It's not like it's some fading crush."

Even though he was seventeen, the kid was making a lot of sense. Raelyn was kind and understanding, and I knew she would really want me to be happy.

Ashton continued, "You have always said that Raelyn is a friend that became family. If things work out with Owen, she really would be. You should start with that when you talk to her."

"You know what? That's not bad advice; I just might."

CHAPTER FOURTEEN

Journal Entry

Speaking with Ashton made me feel better. I know we began our conversation with me wanting to help him and make him feel better, but I may have left feeling more enlightened than him. Not only does it warm my heart that he opened up to me about everything with Riley and the struggles he has been going through, which led me to feel like I was needed and trusted by him, but he also made me see that I really should not be overly afraid of sharing my feelings with Raelyn about her brother. I'm still nervous about bringing it up and how I will do so, but Ashton is right. She is such a good friend to me, seriously like family, and she supports me. If she has any problem at all with me forming a deeper relationship with Owen, it will be valid, and I know she'll back it up with reasoning. Where we go from there, I'm not sure. God, please help Rae understand that this could be a good thing here, an amazing thing. I need her to. So, I pray. I pray for that, and I pray for my little brother, that he finds his way. It's hard *enough trying to figure out who you are in high school, without the added inner conflict of discovering your sexual identity. I'll be there for him though, with every step.*

CHAPTER FIFTEEN

J anuary was nearly over, and I still had not spoken with Raelyn. I knew the conversation was coming soon though. I could feel it. I had been having dreams lately about her reactions to me not confiding in her sooner, which was par for the course with my anxiety. I had built the conversation up so much in my head, that it was starting to seem bigger than it had to be. *Just do it already.*

It was Saturday, so I decided to call her up and invite her out for drinks. Owen and I had talked about possibly telling her together, but then we thought it might be better for me to have my own conversation with her and for him to reach out afterward.

Raelyn let me pick, so I chose a little lounge on Main Street in New Hope. We met there, which was good, just in case she was not very receptive to the news and didn't feel like driving home with me. I was counting on a positive outcome, but I had learned in the past to never be too sure.

We ordered our favorite martinis and caught up with events from the past month. I thanked her again for hooking me up with the ski resort job.

"How was that, by the way? I didn't get a chance to talk to Owen after. Did you guys manage to have any fun?" Raelyn had given me the perfect opening.

As I was about to tell her about our weekend, the waitress brought two more martinis to our table. We were only halfway through our firsts.

"I think you have the wrong table. We have not ordered more drinks yet," I told her nicely.

"I know; they are from that gentleman sitting at the bar with the white shirt. Enjoy!" The waitress left, and we tried to get a good look at who she was referring to. When I finally saw his face, I was thrown. I leaned in close to Raelyn.

"That's him, Rae," I said in a loud whisper.

"Who? What are you talking about?" she whispered back to me.

"The guy, the one from my aunt and uncle's holiday party. That's Marcelo." This was a very odd coincidence.

"No way? We have to get him over here!" Rae signaled for Marcelo to join us before I could stop her.

Accepting the invitation, he politely asked the couple at the next table if he could take one of their empty stools and pulled it up to ours. When he sat down, all I could do was smile and sip my drink.

"So, I was thinking of giving you a call. I guess I have been trying to muster up the courage." That was a lame excuse, but the truth was that I really didn't care. He was an attractive and charming guy, but I hadn't really wanted to hear from him.

"No worries at all. Things have been hectic anyway for me," I said.

"I'm Raelyn, by the way!" Rae interjected kindly and held out her hand to shake his.

I jumped in, "Where are my manners? I am so sorry. Marcelo, this is my best friend, Raelyn. Rae, this is Marcelo. He is a friend and coworker of my cousin, Ryan."

"You can call me Marc," he said.

"Well, Marc, it's nice to meet you. I understand you recently met Sophia at a family party. Is she not the greatest?" Raelyn was such a sweetheart; she always talked me up to people.

"She most definitely is." Marcelo looked at me with a flirtatious grin.

"Both of you are making me blush. Cut it out." My cheeks warmed as they turned three shades of red.

Marcelo stayed for a couple of drinks with us and then filled us in on some of his favorite local hot spots. He even suggested we join him at one when we were ready to leave the lounge. I could tell that Rae was reeling at the thought of me dating Marc, and she softly kicked me under the table to tell me to say yes to continuing the night with him. I brought her out tonight to confess my feelings for her brother, and now we were hanging out with another guy who she hoped I was interested in.

"Sure! We would love to," I said.

How was I going to explain this to Owen?

"I can go for one drink, but then I have to be getting home. I have a very early start tomorrow morning." "Oh yeah? A Sunday photo shoot?" Marcelo asked.

"Yes, I am doing some engagement pictures for a couple I know." It was true that I had to work tomorrow. I just did not have to start until noon.

"One drink it is then," Rae said excitedly.

One drink, and that's it. I mean it.

We walked down the street about two blocks to a corner pub. I had seen this place on my travels through New Hope, but I had never gone in. Once we were inside, Marcelo found us some seats at the bar and signaled to a bartender, who he appeared to be familiar with.

"Hey Marc! I see you are with two beautiful ladies tonight.

I'm Nick, a friend of his," he said to us. "Here's a food and drink menu."

We all decided to have a beer, since we were in a pub, and we were trying to choose an appetizer to split between the three of us.

"Irish nachos are highly recommended!" Nick said.

That did not take much convincing. We all looked at each other and nodded. *Yum!*

While we waited for the food, Rae asked Marcelo what seemed like a hundred questions. I respected it though; she wanted to see what type of guy I could potentially be going out with. He took it like a champ too, making us both laugh at every turn.

"I became an accountant so I would always feel depreciated," Marcelo said.

"I cannot!" I said, chuckling.

"You are funny, Marc!" Raelyn encouraged him. "I like you! We should all get together sometime with my husband, Kevin."

Stop, Rae. Please stop.

"I will text you right now, Sophia, so that you have my number. You can reach out when and if the three of you would like to go out sometime. Does that sound good?" Marcelo asked.

"That sounds perfect." *It really didn't, but what else was I to say?*

We used the bathroom and parted ways with him. I was suddenly feeling disappointed that I did not have my talk with Raelyn, but I supposed it would have to wait until another time. I was exhausted and needed my bed.

Rae and I parked in the same lot, so we hugged when we got there and walked to our own cars. I told her she needed to come over to hang on her next free night, and that was the way that I left it. I assured myself that Owen would have to understand that there was an obstacle. *How would I explain that particular obstacle though?*

When I returned home, I quickly scooted up to my bedroom, calling for Harley. She came running out of my parents' bedroom and hopped up onto my bed. She curled herself against the pillows by my head.

"Let's go to sleep, pretty girl."

CHAPTER SIXTEEN

I woke up the next morning, and I stretched my right arm out to cuddle Harley, but she was not there. *Not this again.*

I sat up and scanned the room. I was shocked to see Harley laying on the floor next to the bed on the shaggy carpet.

"Girl, why are you not up here with me?"

She stared at me, and she wagged a little, but something was not right. I climbed down and sat next to her.

"What's wrong?" I petted her fur to comfort her and kissed her forehead. Fear consumed me. *Maybe she ate something.*

"Har, I will be right back." I went to see if my mom and dad were awake yet. Their door was shut, but I heard my dad talking. I knocked and asked if one of them could help me. My dad opened the door to see what the problem was.

"Dad, something is off with Harley. Come to my room." I grabbed his arm and pulled him with me.

When he saw Harley on the floor, he sat down next to her and agreed something was off. Suddenly, I noticed that her face looked droopy on her left side.

"Dad, do you see how one side of her mouth is saggy?

What do you think happened? I'm scared. Do you think she's having an allergic reaction?" I was in full panic mode and felt an anxiety attack coming on. Pains were forming in my chest, and my fingers were suddenly numb.

"Sophia, I'm going to call the vet now to see if we can get an appointment right away. I'm not sure what happened, but they should be able to tell us. Try to relax." Dad was always able to remain calm in stressful situations. I admired that in him and was equally jealous at the same time. I have had an anxiety disorder since I was in elementary school, and while I have learned from past experiences, I still struggled when the unknown presented itself.

"I am taking her down for some water, and I will get her comfy by the fireplace. Thanks for calling the doctor, Dad." It was Sunday, so it was possible they wouldn't be able to see her until the next day.

"I will call the emergency line too, but there is no guarantee. While you are in the kitchen, you might want to take a Lorazepam to calm down." Dad knew me better than anyone in our family. I only took that when my anxiety was overpowering, but it happened enough that I needed to have a prescription.

I filled Harley's water bowl and took my medicine. Next, I guided her into the living room and laid out a blanket in front of the fireplace. I added her favorite stuffed animal, a lion cub, and helped her get comfy. So many thoughts were racing through my mind. *Is this a bee sting? Is she sick? Did she have some type of stroke during the night? What happened to her?*

Of course, I began searching for it on my laptop, which you should never do. Some websites will tell you your dog has a week left to live, based on any given symptoms. I then typed into Google everything that I could think of, from saggy lips on a dog to paralysis of the face. I found a ton of information, but not much of it was uplifting. Mostly, I read that I should contact my vet right away. I knew they would have answers for us. It was just a matter of when she could be seen.

As I was sitting on the floor with my head in my computer and my left hand on Harley, Dad came down with Mom to give me an update about the vet.

"The doctor's office is closed, so I left a voicemail, but one of the doctor's called me back within five minutes. They must get an alert when someone leaves a message," Dad informed me.

"Honey, the doctor said we can bring Harley in first thing tomorrow morning and that we should monitor her symptoms and give her a lot of water until then. Your father went into detail about the symptoms, and they said it could be a number of things, one even being a bad ear infection." Mom had such a nice, calming voice when she was reporting news.

"Thanks, Dad. You too, Mom," I said to both of them. "I know we just have to be patient until tomorrow. Maybe it is an infection that will just need antibiotics."

"You go to work, and we will stay with her all day." Mom told me and then ushered me away.

I guessed there was no sense in the three of us sitting with her right then, four if Ashton woke up and wanted to stay by her side too. I went up and put myself together for my shoot and headed out. All I could think about the whole time though was what could be wrong with my little nugget.

After work, I came home and snuggled up next to Harley, watching television until it was time to go to bed, and then I brought her up to my bedroom with me.

The next morning, I was up before sunrise. I could not sleep well, the worry seeping deeper and deeper into my gut, and I wanted us to be the first people at the doctor's office so

Harley could be seen as soon as possible. We sat in the waiting room until the nurse called us into a patient room. Ashton had school, so both Mom and Dad went with me to have the vet check her out.

"When was the first you noticed a change in her face?" the doctor asked.

"I noticed it yesterday morning when I woke up and then called both of my parents to see."

"Did Harley eat anything she was not supposed to?" the doctor continued.

"Not that we are aware of," Dad replied.

"Well, it could be an allergic reaction to food or a foreign substance, or she could have been bitten by something. Another possibility is that she may have a severe inner ear infection. sometimes they can cause temporary facial nerve paralysis."

"Whatever tests you need to run, go right ahead. We need to get some answers!" Mom responded to the doctor frantically.

"I am going to check her for a rash or a bite, and I will check her ears and run a culture test. The plan of action will be to rule out one thing at a time." The doctor began assessing Harley for other side effects that could be connected to an allergic reaction from a bite, food, or something unknown. We watched in anticipation.

"She does not appear to be having an allergic reaction, but I am going to send you home with a two-day treatment that will reduce the swelling if she is experiencing anything of the sort." This update from the doctor mildly relieved me, but then he began checking her ears.

"Her right ear looks healthy, aside from some wax that we can clean out before you go. I do see some inflammation inside her left ear though. Yes, it is very red, which would definitely explain the facial distortion on that same side of her head."

"What does this mean?" Dad asked.

"Without having definitive results back from the lab of her culture that I am taking, my professional opinion is that Harley has an inner ear infection. I am prescribing medicated drops that will need to be administered twice a day, as well as an antibiotic and a very strong steroid that will have to be taken with her food in the morning. I will expect to see her back here in two weeks to evaluate her progress."

We left the vet with some piece of mind. Hopefully, this was just an ear infection causing the facial distortion. The only thing to do was wait.

February had reared its ugly head. In my opinion, it was the worst month of them all. Not only is work usually slow, but my anxiety was at the highest peak in February every year. My physician said it's because of the lack of vitamin D in the winter due to little sunlight, which causes Seasonal Affective Disorder (SAD) and can lead to a deeper anxiety and depression. He recommended that I get an indoor sun lamp to supplement, but I had yet to do so. I was the only one in my family that had been diagnosed with an anxiety disorder, but I was starting to think Ashton might be falling into a depression.

That week, he confided in me that Riley had been acting distant ever since the night Ashton kissed him. I had feared that Riley would be uncomfortable hanging out with Ashton at first, but it appeared he was having trouble getting over the situation. I told him I believed the friendship would survive if it was strong enough. Sadly, I didn't have much better advice to give. The reality was Ashton had feelings for Riley that were not being reciprocated, and that was a hard pill to swallow, but it was a life lesson as well.

"I am so miserable, Soph! I hate my life," Ashton said.

"Ashton, you cannot hate your life just because Riley does not feel the same way about you. He is straight, and you...you are not completely. That is as good a reason as any to not take something personal and be offended."

"It's not just that. Riley was my only good friend, and now I have nobody. School is the worst, and I don't even know what team I am playing for anymore." Ashton may not have meant to be funny, but I had to smile at his last comment.

"Buddy, I am sure you have at least one or two other friends between your classes and your job. If not, you have a big family who loves you no matter what, and you are going away to college in less than a year. Do not let a temporary situation put you in a dark place." I tried to help him see how much better things would be in just six months or so.

"I don't know. Everything just makes me so sad lately. All I want to do is lay in bed and pull the blanket over my head and stay there," Ashton grumbled.

"Keeping to yourself in your room is not healthy. You cannot shut the world out. This is your senior year, and you will regret it later if you do not try to enjoy what is left of it."

As I was telling him to make the best of things in his last year of high school, thinking I was really getting through to him, I was knocked off course by a disturbing sight. My eyes widened.

"Sophia, what is it?" Ashton asked.

I must have had a horrified look on my face.

Ashton had rolled up the sleeves to his sweatshirt to reveal marks that should not have been there, and they definitely would not be there by accident.

"Tell me it has not been going on long," I pleaded with him.

"What? What are you even talking about?" He questioned me, seeming very unaware.

"Ashton, this is serious. Please, you...you cannot harm yourself."

He realized what I had seen, snatched back his arm, and pulled his sleeves back down.

"I...I just did it a couple of times recently. I won't do it again." His eyes shifted quickly as he spoke, and he scratched at his neck, his age-old tell.

"Ashton, I can see that some of those marks are older. When...when did you start cutting yourself?" I gently implied I knew he was not being honest.

He sat silent in the chair staring at the carpet.

"Ashton, talk to me. When?"

"November...I started doing it in November." His eyes filled with tears.

I grabbed some tissues from the box on the end table and put them in his hand. I rubbed his back and stood there for a minute while he let it out.

"Ash, what provoked you to do it that first time?"

"I was not trying to slit my wrists. I swear it. I was just trying to cause enough pain to make me forget about everything else going on. We had an assembly at the beginning of the school year about suicide and self-harm. The speaker shared with us how he used to cut himself on his arms and his thighs when he was my age. Apparently, the physical pain relieved his mental and emotional pain. While what the guy was saying was supposed to teach us not to do it, I couldn't stop thinking about whether it would do the same for me. So, one day while I was sitting in my room upset, I tried it," Ashton explained.

"This is not the way you deal with mental and emotional pain. That speaker was there to educate all of you about depression and the proper avenues for coping. Cutting into your body for a momentary fix is not one of them!" I was getting worked up, and he knew it.

More tears flooded from Ashton's face.

"I know! I just...I don't know what to do. I cannot deal with myself. I am up all night wondering when it is that I will start to feel better. You don't know what it's like to feel isolated and to feel like you don't know who you are."

I scooted closer to him and took his hand in mine. "I never struggled with my sexual identity, no, but you know how severe my anxiety has been. Anxiety and depression are very closely connected. They are both a result of a chemical imbalance in the brain or the result of trauma. With the right support, you can learn to love yourself and have a life that feels normal."

"When you say the right support, you mean therapy?" Ashton asked.

"Yes, I mean therapy, but I also mean the support of my amazing family and good friends. I have two prescriptions to aid in keeping me balanced too." I was willing to share details of my experiences if it helped him gain insight.

"You don't go to therapy now, do you?"

"Not currently, Ash, but I went in high school and a few years back again. I have attended individual and group counseling. I was apprehensive about the group sessions at first because I didn't want to share with strangers, but it was beneficial to hear others share their problems. I related to what they were dealing with, which made me feel like I was not alone. I would recommend group counseling to anyone."

"How come you have not been going lately? Are you healed?" Ashton asked me innocently.

"I am not healed. Having a mental illness can be a lifelong journey, but I stopped going to therapy because I found the right dosage of anti-anxiety medication. I take it every single day, and it really helps me deal. I still get anxious about the unknown, but I don't exhibit the behaviors I used to, like over analyzing, being obsessive compulsive, and having regular panic attacks."

"Your medicine helps with all of that? Do you think medicine would help me with being depressed all of the time?"

"I mean, I can't say for certain since everyone is different. But it really has worked wonders for me. I would say it would not hurt you to see a doctor about possibly taking an antidepressant. However, I think some type of therapy is in order here too. Self-harm can sometimes lead to more drastic measures, and I refuse to entertain any scenarios where that happens with you."

"Do I go to therapy at school? What if other kids find out I go?"

"Trust me, there are more kids at your school that participate in one type of counseling or another than you are aware of. Most of them don't talk about it because they are worried about what everyone else will think or say, just like you. That's what the counselors are there for though, to help students with anxiety, erratic behavior, depression, issues at home, and whatever else is causing a disruption to their education and mental health." I knew all of this from being one of those kids.

"I guess I can give it a try. At least, I am halfway through my last year, so if I do feel humiliated, I won't have to face the other kids for much longer."

Ashton agreed to see a school counselor, and I was so proud of him for both listening to my advice and being willing to accept help. The next step was to tell Mom and Dad, and they already had their minds consumed with worry over Harley.

CHAPTER SEVENTEEN

Harley had been taking the medicine the vet prescribed for nearly two weeks, but there had been no improvement. Her face still looked like it had nerve paralysis, and she was now digging at her left ear with her paw sporadically. *Poor girl!*

We were all trying not to worry, as the doctor said it could take several weeks to completely eliminate the ear infection. Dad was going to take her for her two-week follow-up appointment on the thirteenth, and we would go from there. *How was it almost Valentine's Day already?*

I didn't have plans for the holiday yet, but in my mind, I saw a lengthy, romantic, secluded date with Owen. Spending the night with him seemed feasible. I just didn't know if I could enjoy it without being transparent with Raelyn first. I had recently spoken with her when I called her to tell her about Harley, but that was not the right time to bring up her brother.

Just as I was thinking I would probably end up alone on Valentine's Day, Owen called.

"Hey! How's my favorite furry friend doing over there?" Owen asked in a playful but concerned tone.

"She's hanging in there, but she hasn't made any progress yet. My dad is taking her to her next appointment in a couple of days, so I'm trying to stay calm until then." The fact that the first thing he mentioned was Harley melted my heart. Owen doted on her like she was the only animal in this world, which was another quality that I admired about him. If he acted that way with a dog, making her feel so special without even trying, I knew he would be a devoted husband one day.

"Well, you said it could take weeks before she's better. The infection could be on its way out but will continue to show signs until it's gone."

"You could be right. How have you been doing? Any new gigs?" I didn't think of him as my competition in the area because I wanted him to be successful as well.

"I lined up a couple for the second half of this month and one in March so far. Rae said her boss has more work for me too. You?"

"I have a few things in the works too, and Rae also sent me information about work at her magazine. I wondered if we would end up on the same job again." My voice lifted at the end of the sentence, an energy of hopefulness coursing through it.

"That could be a lot of fun!" Owen said. "Actually, one of the reasons I called you was that I wanted to see if you had any plans for Friday night."

"This Friday? You mean Valentine's Day? Yup, I have two dates back to back. I'm not sure how I'll pull it off," I joked.

"That's a real shame. I wanted to take you out."

"You snooze, you lose." I bit my lip to suppress a laugh.

"Is one of the dates with your new guy, Marc?" Owen asked, his voice flecked with a tinge of jealousy.

"What? How do you know that name, and what makes you think he is my new guy?" Raelyn must have told him that we ran into him.

94

"My sister and I do chat sometimes, Soph." He laughed and then continued. "She told me all about that night in New Hope and how she wants to set up a double date for you and him to join her and Kevin." I suddenly felt sick.

"We ended up being at the same bar with him, and then the three of us hung out for a little, but I have no intentions of seeing him again. That's not where my head is." There was a silent pause, and then Owen broke it with a bold assertiveness.

"Where exactly is your head?"

"Owen, I think you are fully aware of where my interest lies, or more importantly, with whom. I have made my feelings pretty clear, haven't I?"

"Maybe, but it's still nice to hear." I could tell he was smiling on the other end of the phone.

"I was just kidding before, you know, about having plans on Friday night. I am totally free." I figured he already knew that, but I had to confirm.

"Whew! That's a relief. Can I take you out then?"

How could I say no to Owen? I couldn't. I wouldn't.

"I would be honored to be your date Friday night," I replied happily.

"Great! Let me know what Raelyn says when you tell her." I could feel the sarcasm in his voice.

"Very funny, Owen! Hey, maybe *you* should be the one to talk to her first. After all, she is your family." I attempted to wriggle off the hook, even though I knew I would have had to have the dreaded conversation with her eventually anyway.

"I am fine with speaking to Rae about it. I just thought you wanted to feel her out before I did. She's your best friend, and I don't want to jeopardize your relationship by saying something she would have wanted to hear from you first." Owen responded, making a valid point.

Before we hung up, I assured him I would get in touch with her and dive into the matter at hand. Like a Band-Aid, it wasn't going to be easy or comfortable, but at some point, I was just going to have to rip it off once and for all.

I went to the kitchen to fetch a small bottle of merlot and a wine glass. I needed to calm my nerves before attempting the conversation with Rae. Only Mom was downstairs, lounging on the black leather recliner in the living room, deep into one of her romance novels. I said a quick hello and darted back up to my bedroom to secure some privacy to contact Rae.

I picked up my cell from my wooden desk in the corner of my room, where I had left it after my call with Owen. When I shifted the lock screen upward, I saw that there were two unread text messages. One was from Owen, wishing me luck with a thumbs-up emoji and a kiss emoji at the end. Ironically, the other was from Raelyn, suggesting we set plans up this weekend for that double date with Marcelo and Kevin. I had to talk to her.

She picked up after the first ring, and I knew this was it.

"Rae! I just saw your message. I was planning on calling you tonight actually. How is it going over there?" I was warming up.

"I can't complain, Soph. Any updates on my girl?"

"Huh?" *Is she talking about me?* "What kind of updates? What do you mean?" *Does she know?*

"Are there updates on Harley since the other day when we talked?" she asked, ignoring my frenetic state.

"Oh, no. Nothing has changed yet, but I'll be sure to keep you posted. Thanks for asking."

"Of course, I worry about that big yellow fluff ball," Raelyn laughed, showing she was in a good mood. *Thank goodness!*

"Listen, about your text..." I led into it.

"It's perfect, right? We go on a double date on Valentine's Day weekend! I mean, if he's available that is." She was over the moon now about me and this guy.

"Rae, I don't think we should go out with Marcelo." *Here it comes.*

"Why, Soph? Would you rather just go out with him yourself instead of with all of us?"

"No, that's not it. I...I do not want any of us to go out with him," I told her.

"I'm confused. Do you not like Marc for some reason?" she asked.

"No, I don't. Not in that way," I admitted.

"Really? I am so sorry. I wasn't trying to push him on you. It just really seemed like you had a good vibe with him." Though Raelyn apologized, being the doll that she is, it was me who felt bad for not being honest with her from the beginning.

"There's no reason to be sorry. The truth is, and I have been meaning to tell you, that I sort of...well, I have feelings for someone else, but I have been too afraid to admit it to anyone." I was at the point of no return.

"Sophia! Who? Do I know them? I cannot believe it!" Raelyn's voice became high pitched.

"You know him," I mumbled.

"I do? From where?"

"Are you sitting down, Rae?" *Please be sitting down.*

"Why do I need to be sitting down? Are you seeing one of my exes? Sophia, spit it out!"

Just rip the Band-Aid off.

"Raelyn, no! I'm not dating one of your exes. I would never do that."

"Just tell me. Please?"

"It's Owen." I took a deep breath in and let it out slowly.

"Owen? Owen who? My brother? You have feelings for my brother?"

"Yes!" I blurted out before falling into silence.

"Since when? How did this happen?" Rae asked impatiently.

"I don't know. I've always found him very good-looking and interesting. He makes me laugh, and he gets me, and there seems to be more of a connection than a friendship now."

"Did this start when you two were in the Poconos, Soph?"

"No, it has been developing for a little while now. I just didn't want to do anything about it unless you were okay with us spending time together." I really hoped she would understand.

"So, you're telling me nothing at all has happened between you and my brother yet?"

"Not even a kiss, Rae!"

"Well, what the hell are you two waiting for?" she asked me, raising her voice a bit.

"Wait? Are you serious?"

"Yes! If you are into him, and he is into you, don't let me hold you back. I am here for it!"

"Really? It wouldn't bother you to have your best friend dating your brother?"

"Sophia, why would you even think that? I could not choose anyone better for Owen. Plus, if things worked out, you could maybe end up being my sister-in-law!" *I should've started out with that, like Ashton said!*

"Wow! I have to admit I am pleasantly surprised by your reaction, Rae. I guess I assumed you would disapprove because of my relationship with you. Like, what if things don't work out with me and him? What happens to us then?" I needed her to see the entire picture.

"I hope our friendship is strong enough that we would be able to overcome any challenges you and Owen might face." Raelyn's faith mollified my anxiety.

"I believe it is. Thank you for being supportive!"

"Of course, I will always support you!" Raelyn said. "So, does this mean you already have a date for Valentine's Day?"

"I guess I do!" I smiled against the phone, eager to phone Owen with the good news. "Oh, and Rae, I love you."

I hung up with her to call Owen and confirm our plans for Friday night.

CHAPTER EIGHTEEN

Dad took Harley to her follow-up appointment and came home with an update. The doctor said that she should continue with the antibiotic and steroid and then scheduled her for three weeks out to reevaluate. Apparently, severe inner ear infections can take multiple rounds of treatment. Since her status has not changed, we thought it was time to do a family Zoom session to inform the others.

I sent out the invitation to everyone in our immediate family. I then sent a follow-up text in our family group chat to remind them to go to their emails and click on the link. I gave everyone two hours to clear some time to be there, and when my alarm on my phone went off on the hour, I began the Zoom meeting. Paityn was the first to arrive, and then Elijah, and the rest of the family followed after. I stayed in my bedroom to host the meeting, and Ashton stayed in his. Mom and Dad joined from the family room, where Harley was nearby and could make a guest appearance if she liked. Oliver attended the meeting from his work.

Even though I was the host, Dad was the one to let

everyone know that we had important news. I was glad I wasn't the one to have to say it, as I was sure many tears would come halfway through the talk. Everyone remained unmuted so they could react without fidgeting with the computer.

"A member of the James family has become ill. Do not be alarmed, as we are hoping for a recovery sooner than later and still have some avenues to explore." Dad mentally prepared my siblings.

"What? Who is sick?" Oliver expressed a reasonably high level of concern.

"Mom, did something happen?" Elijah inquired, just as worried.

Paityn sat with Liam on her lap and a look of shock on her face. She was frozen, and not for technological reasons, and she was surely expecting Dad to say that it was him or Mom that was sick.

"Please try to calm down. Mom and I are fine. It's Harley that is not okay," Dad said solemnly.

"What's wrong with her?" Paityn asked, as her face changed to uncertain fear. The whole Zoom room was quiet for a moment.

"As of right now, she has an inner ear infection that refuses to go away. The doctor says it can take several rounds of treatment, but the time has come for all of you to know, since there has not been any progress," Mom added to the discussion.

"She has an inner ear infection, and antibiotics aren't working at all?" Paityn asked to make sure she understood.

"Yes, exactly...so, we are beginning to think it could be something more. We just won't know for sure until she sees the vet again."

Nobody spoke for what felt like a minute, even though in

reality, it was more like ten seconds. Then, I finally decided I was going to break the silence with a little bit of positivity.

"The good news is that she is under the care of an excellent doctor, and we have been taking her in often to be evaluated. If it is something more serious, there might be a treatment for that as well. Let's try not to get worked up until we know more information. As soon as we know, all of you will know too!"

I saw a few looks of despair from the faces of my family and a few looks of hope. I spoke the truth though; all we could do is wait and pray for the best outcome. It was easier said than done, I knew. I should have taken my own advice of not stressing about things until I had to, but I felt like maybe this would teach me to do so.

We ended the Zoom meeting right after we briefly did a family member check-in. This was where each individual takes a moment to share or update the rest of the clan. No major news was disclosed, but Oliver did tell us how smitten he was still with Chloe, which was a boost to our spirits after the somber conversation. *Thank goodness he found her.*

———

Friday night had finally arrived, and in typical Sophia fashion, no pun intended, I was altogether indecisive about what to wear for my date with Owen. I changed my attire three times, shoes included, and stared at myself in the floor length mirror inside my walk-in closet. I didn't know how I would ever give up this closet when it was time for me to move out. I considered the temperature, both inside and outside of any given restaurant, and eventually chose a three-quarter sleeve, deep red, form-fitting dress that reached my knees. I paired it with short heeled, black closed-toe shoes and added some gold jewelry and a black purse. My dark gray pea coat looked perfect with the ensemble, and I was ready only minutes before he rang the doorbell.

When I opened the front door, Owen was standing there in navy blue slacks and a sport jacket to match, a button-down pale-yellow shirt with no tie, and brown Berluti shoes. This guy knew how to dress to impress. *Do not stare too much.*

"You look beautiful." Owen complimented me in the most genuine, adoring way.

"You clean up pretty well yourself." I smiled at him, while admiring his outfit. "I am digging the shoes!"

"Thanks. Shall we go?" He held out his arm for me to hook into, and we walked to his car.

Owen, being the gentleman that he was, opened my door for me to get in. We pulled away, and this feeling of elation was taking over, accompanied by butterflies in my stomach.

"Where are we going? Can I know yet?" He wanted it to be a surprise.

"I think I'll just let you slowly figure it out as we get closer," he replied.

I could tell we were headed in the direction of New Hope, which was only a fifteen-minute drive from my house, but I still didn't have an inkling of the place. We entered the town, but Owen continued to drive.

"Is it not in New Hope?" I asked him, hoping he would give in this time.

"You are getting warm, Soph!"

As we approached the New Hope-Lambertville Bridge, I knew where he must be taking me. *How romantic!*

We drove over the bridge, and Owen glanced sideways at me, checking to see if I knew.

"Owen, are we going to the Lambertville Station?"

He grabbed my left hand with his right hand and flashed a huge grin.

We made a right into the parking lot immediately after we

exited the bridge, and all I could do was smile. *I've always wanted to come here.*

Once the server took our order, Owen dove into how relieved he was that we did not have to hide anything about our relationship from his sister anymore, and I shared the same delight over the freedom from that particular apprehension.

As dinner moved forward, I noticed Owen staring at me...a lot. I tried to brush it off at first, but then I realized I was staring into his baby blues just as much.

"Sophia, I would like to see where things could go between us. How do you feel about that?" Owen was leaning in and reaching for my hand across the table.

"I might be interested in seeing where things go." I smiled and winked at him. "Of course, I feel the same way, Owen."

"You know, I have been taken with your beauty ever since we first met." Owen told me this, assuming I'd known all along.

"That's not true. You have barely batted an eye at me," I replied modestly.

"Seriously, I had to discreetly steal glances at you every time you were around so that you wouldn't catch me and think I was a creep."

"I don't believe you!" I nudged his arm playfully.

"It's true. I would never lie to you." He squeezed my hand and looked deeply into my eyes. "Have you ever thought of me that way, you know, before recently?"

"No, not at all." I tried to keep a straight face.

"Really?" He responded with uncertainty.

"Well, maybe I thought you were attractive." I smirked at him, which blew my cover. "Owen, I have always thought of you in that way. I was just too scared to do anything about it."

"Was this fear because of Rae or because of me?"

"I suppose it was equally distributed between the two of you."

"I hope you are not scared anymore." He continued to gaze into my eyes intensely.

"My fears are gone." I covered his hand on the table with both of mine. A song came on that was familiar to both of us. It was "Heaven" by Kane Brown.

"Would you like to dance with me?" Owen slid out his chair from our table, stood up, and held out his hand for me. There were only two other couples on the dance floor, but I was not passing up the opportunity to have my body against his, moving in slow motion.

"I would love to!" I said to him excitedly.

His arms wrapped around my waist, and all I could think was how long I had wanted to feel like this. I now had my hands folded behind his neck, looking at his jawline, his eyes, his cheekbones, and his full lips.

Kiss me, Owen.

"Heaven" concluded and transitioned to "All of Me" by John Legend.

Owen ran his hands through the curled ends of my long hair, moved them down my back, and pulled me in. As the song played *"love your curves and all your edges,"* he softly kissed me, while keeping his right hand anchored on the small of my back.

He released his lips from mine and whispered in my ear.

"We should go outside. I want to show you something."

After slipping into our coats, Owen led me out the side door, down the stone path, and onto the bridge. He wrapped his arms around me from behind.

"I'll keep you warm. Look at this view."

I'm taking it all in.

A few moments later, he took my hand and began leading me further out and then paused.

"Do you see what it says below us?" He pointed to the ground, where there was a line separating the two states, with Pennsylvania written on one side and New Jersey on the other.

"I have been on this bridge before and never stood here," I told him.

"I'm glad your first time is with me then!"

Owen kissed me again, right there, but this time, it was with every ounce of passion that I knew he had and knew the both of us would have together.

"Wow, Owen." Beyond that, I was speechless.

CHAPTER NINETEEN

Journal Entry

Owen and I kissed. We finally *kissed*. And it was better than I imagined it would be.

First, we kissed to one of the most romantic songs, and then we kissed while we were standing in two states simultaneously. Does it get better? God, thank you!

It almost feels too good to be true that I actually have a shot with Owen. After all of this time, I want to pinch myself to see if I'm dreaming.

But I can't get my hopes too high. We only had one date. One amazing date. I don't even know if he and I are truly compatible as a couple. What if we don't communicate the best when a problem arises? What if we find out things about each other we never knew and don't like those discoveries? I have to be prepared for that, just in case. I can't have unrealistic expectations that we are just going to float off into the sunset and live happily ever after without any challenges or surprises. Anything could happen. And we promised each other that no *matter what, we would make sure to hold on tight to our friendship. I'm not willing to give that up. I'm not willing to give him up, even if it means we don't end up together.*

CHAPTER TWENTY

Owen and I spent a considerable amount of time together over the next couple of weeks trying to get to know each other as more than friends, and things between us were evolving well.

I wish I could have said the same for Harley. There was still no change in her appearance, even though she had gone through two rounds of medication and was about to start her third round. *There has to be more going on here.*

To add to the stress in the James' household, Ashton had begun his individual therapy sessions with one of the school counselors, Mrs. Whitman, but he still had me keeping his secret from Mom and Dad.

One evening, I caught him studying at his computer desk as I was walking by and thought I would try to give him some encouragement for opening up.

"Hey, Ash! How is school going?"

"It's okay. Each day, we get closer to the end, so that's a positive."

"And how is therapy going?" I pried a little more.

"It's been good actually." He bent down to the floor to

unzip his backpack. "I like Mrs. Whitman. After we discussed my depression and what I had been doing to deal with it, she did some exercises with me to help me find healthy ways to cope with my stress, anxiety, and depressive states. Obviously, none of them will involve self-harm or shutting down."

"Are you keeping a list on that notepad you removed from your school bag?" I noticed some writing scrawled on his papers. I was curious to know what he was learning and if he'd tried any of her recommendations yet.

"She has me write during every session. It's one of the coping strategies I've been working on. There are others in here too, yeah."

"What are some strategies she suggested?" I didn't want to invade his privacy by asking to see, so I rested a hand on his shoulder, hoping he would feel comfortable enough to open up.

"Well, writing is one of them, so I have pages filled in this book. I write at home too. Another is saying my thoughts out loud to other people that I trust, which is why she wanted me to start group therapy right away – to start fostering a rapport with some of the other kids in there so that I feel more willing to speak up more. There are a bunch. Here, read them." He handed me his notepad.

The list included methods I had both seen and applied. His counselor advised him to refer to it any time he was feeling closed in, under pressure, down on himself, or isolated.

I read the list aloud, trying to get a sense of which ones Ashton might prefer. "Take a time out, such as trying yoga, meditating, listening to music, or just stepping away to try and clear your head." Ashton nodded his head. "Eat well-balanced meals, and keep energy boosting snacks on hand." Ashton smirked a little as I continued, "Be sure to limit all alcohol and caffeine, which can aggravate anxiety and trigger panic attacks." He nodded again. "Get enough sleep, exercise daily, take deep breaths, accept imperfection, realize that you cannot control everything, welcome humor for good laughs, and maintain a positive attitude." Ashton smiled and reached out his hand to take the book.

"I've been trying some of these, and they do seem to help," Ashton admitted.

"I'm so glad to hear it!" I really was proud of him. Not everyone can admit when they have a problem and then be willing to take the steps to make it better.

"Thanks! There is something else I do have to tell you about," he said.

I was intrigued.

"What is that?" I asked him.

"Riley is in my group therapy. Can you believe that?"

"What? That's...interesting. Did you know he was seeing the counselor?"

"I had no idea! I guess it's like you said before, how many kids go to therapy without anyone else knowing." He really does listen to me when I talk.

"Ashton, to place the two of you in the same group, there must be common issues to a certain extent. You do not have to break any confidentiality, but do you want to tell me more about it?"

"I have only had two group sessions so far, but it turns out Riley had an issue at his last school that caused him a lot of distress. Whatever it was is still a problem for him. His parents thought counseling would benefit himt. I didn't know he was struggling with anything, Soph. He never talked about it before."

"Did he tell you that individually at therapy or to the group?"

"Well, today was my second session with him, so when it was over, I asked him if I could walk with him to our next class. He said that it would be okay if I did, and that's when it came out. While we were walking, I took the opportunity to apologize for the kiss. I told him how confused I've been in that area of my life and said I was wrong for misreading the signs."

"Wow, Ashton. That was mature of you. So, what did he say?"

"After I explained where my head had been, he told me he shouldn't have run off the way he did, and there was something about him that he had not told me. He said it was the reason he switched schools after junior year. But when I finally thought I was going to get answers, the bell rang."

"What do you think he wanted to tell you?" I could only come up with that he may have gotten into some serious trouble at his previous high school, but I did not share this with Ashton.

"I don't know what it could be, but I assume it has to do with why he reacted the way he did when I kissed him. That night, I thought I was accurately reading all of the signs, every vibe leading up to that moment, but then I concluded that I must have been way off. It would be comforting to know there is a specific reason why he felt he had to dash out of the house like that, other than being totally grossed out by me."

"Keep the communication open with him. I'm sure he will open up to you when he's ready," I assured him.

"I will do that. Hopefully, we can get our friendship back on track."

"It looks like things are headed in a positive direction, Ash."

He smiled brightly and gave me a fist bump. I then went back to my room for the night.

CHAPTER TWENTY-ONE

Ashton proceeded with both his individual and group therapy and showed vast improvements in his mood and disposition over the following weeks, while the opposite was true for Harley. I didn't tell Mom and Dad any of this, but my head was full of doubt for the culprit being an ear infection. I knew the doctor had said it could take a while for the treatments to work, but we were now in the middle of March with zero change in her facial paralysis. What was worse was that Harley's breathing had changed too; she would pant incessantly anytime her medication was wearing off. I read online that when ear infections do not go away with antibiotics, they have to drain the ear, so I started to think maybe the doctor could try that at her next visit.

I considered calling the vet myself to ask about additional alternative treatments when my cell phone lit up.

There was a new text message from Owen: *Hey! I have to speak with you about a job. Can we meet?*

I wrote back suggesting we meet the next day since I had a job myself that evening, taking college team photos for the magazine. As much as I appreciated having the work, I was feeling deflated and drained.

Don't get me wrong, I enjoyed working in different settings on a regular basis and with a variety of people of all ages, but I was having trouble fighting the feeling that I was destined for more.

I wanted to travel and set my own hours, and I dreamed of having my own photography business or being a partner with another owner. I aspired for people to just hear my name one day and know that they did not have to search any further for the photographer of their dreams.

Owen asked if I could meet him for a drink by the train station in Doylestown, and I was eager to hear all there was to know about his new job. Afterall, it was important enough for him to tell me in person rather than over the phone.

Once we were seated and ordered our drafts, Owen began telling me about a new offer that had come in. *Is it not with the magazine? I hadn't been given an assignment.*

"A resort representative who viewed my website asked me to come work for them. Apparently, they called the magazine for a reference, and Rae's boss gave me an excellent review. I'm not sure what made them choose me, but I'm grateful for the opportunity," he explained.

"A resort? Where is it?" I asked.

"It's in North Carolina, in the Outer Banks. They had their grand opening just last week and need someone to photograph the events they have been booking. I leave in a few days."

"Wow! That's...umm, a long drive away, Owen."

"Or a short flight!" he grinned back, his expression hopeful.

"That's true," I conceded, even though a flame of

disappointment ignited in my stomach. "How long will you be gone?"

"It will be for six weeks. Would you want to come with me?" Owen asked.

My mind raced at his question. Did I *want* to go? Of course I did! But how could I? I shook my head, gearing up for the next part. I sighed deeply and blurted out, "I can't go to North Carolina for that long, not now. I have several jobs lined up, and there's too much going on with Ashton and Harley. Easter is right around the corner, and Paityn, Bradley, and Liam are coming again from Georgia. It's...just not a good time." I could see the light in his eyes dim.

"Sure, I hear you. That was selfish of me," Owen replied. He fiddled with his water glass before wiping his wet fingers on the napkin in his lap.

"No, I appreciate the invitation. It makes me feel good to know you would want me to be there with you."

"Well, you can still come for a long weekend if it works with your schedule. I would really like that, a lot."

"I would love that. Will you come back home at all?"

Please say yes.

His eyes were soft and hooded with thick lashes. My stomach dipped when he flashed a smile.

"I am thinking of coming back from that Friday afternoon to Monday morning over the Easter holiday."

I quickly responded by grabbing his hand and giving it a squeeze. "Yes, please!"

"Listen, I know we're still new and all, but I don't want you to worry too much about this. It's only six weeks, and they will fly by, and we will see each other in between." I could see in his expression he was determined to make me feel better.

"I know. It'll be okay. I am very happy for you. This is the longest photography gig you've ever had, and it will look amazing on your resume and your online profile."

"I sure hope so," Owen enthusiastically shot back.

"What about the jobs you have lined up here?" I asked him.

"Fortunately, I only have three jobs set up for the next six weeks, and two of them I can postpone. Would you want to do the other one in my place?

"Sure...send me the details. I should be able to as long as I don't have anything booked," I replied.

"Thank you! I knew I could count on you."

"Of course, but what if you do so well that you keep receiving assignments like this one, where you have to go to other states and work for weeks or for months? Is that where you see the progression of your career?" I asked him honestly.

"That's a great question, and to be honest, I'm not sure if I have an answer for it. I do love to travel, and I want to make a name for myself, but it's complicated because I also envision running my own company. The idea of conducting business on my terms and creating a schedule that works best for me is highly appealing." It seemed like he wanted the same things I did.

"Oh, I can relate. Thoughts of me having my own photography business keep me awake at night. It would make me so much happier than hoping for jobs with Rae's magazine or that word of mouth has spread far enough in the area to land me an abundance of family photo shoots. I want bigger."

"I'm not sure what you mean exactly? Bigger how?"

"I want to be famous for my work. I want people to contact me for their galas, high profile awards ceremonies, celebrity fundraisers, backstage concerts, weddings, and many other events that only established and tremendously talented photographers are hired to do. I want my pictures to be so distinctive, that a person would comment on it being a Sophia James original."

"Wow! I love your passion."

"It might sound like I am a dreamer, Owen, but I have a plan, and this bouncing around from gig to gig is not it."

"Everyone should have dreams, Miss James, and chasing them is what makes life meaningful."

All I could do was smile. I had forgotten about being distraught over his new job at this point. Owen had this remarkable and effortless way of lifting my spirits, and it was one of the reasons I had held on to him so tightly all of these years.

When we left, we promised we would figure out a way to make it work. The only reason I was nervous was because our relationship had been gaining strength with every moment we spent together, and I felt closer to him now than ever before. It had taken us so long to get where we were. What if the distance sets us back?

On the drive home, I concluded I was going to have to trust the process and simply hope for the best. If I was meant to be with Owen, I would be.

I know exactly what I need right now.

I parked my car in the driveway, ran inside, and called for Harley. Snuggles with my girl would make everything better.

CHAPTER TWENTY-TWO

I woke up with a stir about an hour after I had fallen asleep. My arm was stretched out to the side of the bed where Harley always slept, but instead of my fingertips weaving their way through soft fur as expected, I was met with a fistful of cold bed sheets. She was making a habit out of this disappearing act. I sat up, wiped the sleep from my eyes, and scanned my bedroom to see her sitting by the door, heavily panting.

"Hey, baby girl, do you need to go outside?" I asked her while I slid my bare feet into my slippers and tied my robe around my waist with a tight knot.

Harley stood up to follow me downstairs and to the back door. As I waited for her to come back up to the patio, I suddenly remembered I wanted to call her vet and see if it was time for them to try draining her ear. I grabbed the black dry erase marker from the clip on the refrigerator and wrote a note in all capital letters on the magnetic dry erase board hanging there. CALL DOCTOR STANMORE IMMEDIATELY!

I did not want to forget again, and I also wanted my parents to know I was very concerned. An unsettling feeling sat heavy in my gut, and I knew with my whole heart that something just wasn't right.

Harley was pacing all over the patio when I was finished with writing my reminder, so I returned to the door to let her in. I felt so completely helpless. She constantly looked like she was in pain but was trying to be brave about it. I filled her water bowl and then administered some of her ear drops. Next, I sat on the kitchen floor with her, rubbing her back and giving her kisses. It was breaking my heart to see her like this.

"We are going to figure this out, I promise!" As I said the words aloud, tears filled my eyes and streamed down my face. Looking into her big expressive eyes told me everything I was afraid of hearing – this had to be something more serious.

The next morning, I went to the kitchen to grab some coffee and toast and saw that the note I wrote on the board had been circled, and it was now adorned with a large question mark under it. I yelled for my parents, as I had not heard them since I woke up. My dad heard me calling from the garage and instantly came into the house.

"Dad, did we get any more news about Harley? Why did you circle my note on the refrigerator?" I promptly asked him.

"We haven't heard anything new yet. Why do you want to contact the vet? Did something else happen?"

"No! Nothing happened, Dad. That's the problem. Nothing is happening!" I could hear my voice escalating in spite of the fact that I was trying to remain calm. "The steroids and antibiotics are not working. There has been no improvement at all, and in fact, I think she's getting worse."

He put his hands on his hips and nodded solemnly. "Okay, well, try to calm down, and I will give the doctor a call right now."

I sat on one of the tall stools at the counter, sipping my coffee, while Dad was on the phone. I could hear him from the dining room talking with Dr. Stanmore about possibly having her ear drained and asking when we could bring her in. When the conversation ended, Dad announced that we had an appointment for the next day.

Fortunately, my schedule for that following day was clear. Mom and Ashton had work and school, but Dad took the day off so that the two of us could take Harley in together.

When the nurse arrived in the waiting room to collect Harley, she asked for us to both wait while they did the procedure. Of course, we wanted to be there for her, but the doctor surely knew best.

Just over an hour later, the nurse came out and said that the doctor wanted to speak with us and led us back to a room where both he and Harley were.

"Please have a seat," Dr. Stanmore said.

"Was the draining unsuccessful?" Dad asked nervously.

"First, I need you both to understand that the inner ear infection was one theory of what could be causing this trauma with Harley." Dr. Stanmore was prepping us.

"Doctor, are you saying that's not what is wrong with her?" I asked in a rather forward manner.

There was an uncomfortable pause in the room that was broken only by my deep breaths.

"Doc, please, do you now have information that proves it is not an inner ear infection?" Dad persisted for answers.

"Mr. James, Sophia, I am afraid I have some very bad news." I swear my heart broke in two that very second.

The doctor continued in spite of the tears welling in my eyes, "When we went to drain her left ear, we found a large mass inside," Doctor Stanmore said sorrowfully.

"A mass? Like a tumor? Is...is she dying? Just tell us!" I blurted out.

"We are sending it out for a biopsy, and we will not know if the mass is benign or malignant until we receive the images back. I will call you as soon as I have the results."

Once we got to Dad's SUV, he grabbed my hand, and all I could do is cry.

"Honey, there is still a chance it could be benign," Dad said.

"What if it is not? What if it is malignant, and what if her days with us are numbered? I cannot lose Harley, Dad."

"I don't want to lose her either; none of us do. We will smother her with love until, and even after, we hear from the doctor." I could tell Dad was upset too and that he was trying to be strong for me. The entire James family would be beyond devastated if we had to say goodbye to our girl.

Ashton was distraught when we gave him the report, and Mom sobbed throughout the evening. The only way we were going to get through these next couple of days was by doing it together.

The next three days felt like a month. The waiting was unbearable, and as the time ticked on, I couldn't help but assume the worst.

When the doctor finally called Dad's cell phone that Saturday morning, I watched him intently as he accepted the news.

"Thank you, Dr. Stanmore," Dad said, his voice catching in his throat.

"Dad? You can say it. It's malignant, isn't it?" I knew before he answered. I fell to my knees where Harley was sleeping and wrapped my body around her. The sobs came in heavy waves, and I was certain I was going to cry myself dry.

Dad left the living room and came back with Ashton and Mom.

"The mass they found in Harley's left ear is a malignant tumor. Doctor Stanmore said she could live another couple of months with it, and we will have to monitor her quality of life."

"So, we get two more months with her, Dad? That is it?" Ashton asked as tried to hold back from losing it.

"That's the predicted time frame, buddy. I'm so sorry. I don't want this to be true either." Even Dad was struggling to contain his emotions.

Mom spoke with tears in her eyes and a shaky voice, "I think we need to soak up every second of the time we have left with her and show her every day how loved she is."

"We need to let the others know. Isabel, please call Oliver, and I'll call Paityn. Sophia, can you get in touch with Elijah and Bethany?" Dad delegated, and Ashton took my place with Harley, relieved not to have been assigned to anyone.

CHAPTER TWENTY-THREE

The Easter holiday had arrived, and there was more going on than I felt comfortable with. Paityn, Bradley, and Liam were with us for four days, leaving Monday afternoon. Elijah and Bethany would have Easter Sunday brunch at Bethany's mom's house and the second half at our house. Oliver stayed in California with Chloe and her family, but he was planning to come home sometime in late summer. Owen would be here from Saturday to Monday morning, which I was grateful for, but I couldn't keep my thoughts from drifting to the fact that this would be Harley's very last Easter.

I looked back on all of the other holidays since we first had her as a puppy. Her first Halloween with us, she was a pumpkin. She looked so over the top adorable in that costume that we made her a pumpkin every year after. The first Thanksgiving, she could not understand at all why she wasn't eating turkey too, and that concept never really sunk in. It took her until her fifth Independence Day to stop shaking and whining when she would hear fireworks, but she would still hide the minute the first one went off. All of those memories coursed through my mind as I moved through my day.

I supposed I had two options. I could spend the rest of her days in agony, anticipating the hour I would have to say goodbye to my girl forever, or I could choose to spend the remainder of her life smothering her with love. The obvious choice was the latter.

My purse began to vibrate on the granite countertop. I unzipped the front pocket to see my phone beaming with Owen's face. *How does he know when I need him?*

"Hey! How are you?" I answered, attempting to put aside my sadness and muster a delightful tone.

"I'm doing well. How are you holding up?"

"I'm hanging in there. When do you get in? I cannot wait to see your handsome face."

"I should be in Buckingham by noon today, babe. Want to grab lunch at the bistro after I stop home to drop off my bags and see my parents?"

"That sounds perfect, Owen!"

We met inside the French bistro on Cherry Lane that he, Rae, and I used to frequent before Rae met Kevin. Things had changed quite a bit, but Owen recommending this today lifted my mood by bringing back fond memories of good times.

During lunch, we discussed plans of me coming to visit on my birthday weekend and spending a few days with him at the resort. He also shared with me his experiences over the last couple of weeks, highlighting his favorite spots to shoot.

"So, are you going to be with your family all day tomorrow?" Owen did a segue into Easter Sunday.

"Pretty much! I would love for you to come by if you can

fit it in. Rumor has it in the James family that Elijah has some news!" I filled him in on what Paityn recently told me.

"News? What do you think it is?" Owen reacted cheerfully.

"I honestly have no idea. Paityn said she was on the phone with him a few days ago and that he hinted to an update. He would not give her any details though."

"Interesting! Maybe he or Bethany got some kind of promotion or a different position at their jobs? Maybe they got a new pet?" Owen took some guesses.

"It could be either of those, but I am hoping it has something to do with them trying a new treatment to increase their chances of getting pregnant." I reminded Owen of their arduous year with negative test results and the miscarriage.

"That would be a bright light in the dark place your family has been in with Harley."

"Truer words have never been spoken, Owen."

Owen scooted his chair in my direction, leaned in to kiss me on the cheek, and softly told me he would not miss it.

I went home to help prepare dishes and settings for the following day. After several hours of quality family time, our clan attended the Saturday night mass. My favorite part of the service was when Liam was trying to sing along with us. While listening to him, I made a mental note to speak to my sister about him before they left to head back to Georgia on Monday.

My hopes were high to have the chat when we were back home and Liam was asleep, but she and Brad went to bed right along with him, and I was fading fast too. I took Harley and went to my room. *I wonder if she should have him evaluated.*

A repetitive knock and child voice woke me up in the morning, but I could not make out the words. It sounded like Liam was attempting to tell me that the Easter Bunny came. I put my pajama pants on with the tiny gray and pink rabbits on them and a white long-sleeved shirt, and then I tied Harley's carrot bandana around her neck.

"Good morning, Liam! Did he come?" I asked him as I swung the door swiftly open. "Did you wake up Uncle Ashton?"

"So! So! Him come! See!" Liam still could not refer to me by Aunt Sophia or Aunt Soph.

"Yay! Let's get Uncle Ash!" I told him as we walked down the hall to his bedroom door.

"As! Up!" Liam shouted to Ashton.

Paityn then led Liam down the stairs, and we followed behind them. Bradley and my parents must have already been in the kitchen drinking coffee and making breakfast. The three of them were the biggest early birds, unlike my little brother and myself.

Liam climbed on a chair and picked up his and Harley's Easter baskets from the long, dark, wooden dining room table. He brought Harley's to the coffee table and held onto his.

"We open!" Liam said excitedly.

"Here, bud, I will help Harley peek through and choose something, and Mommy can help you. Okay?" I sat on the couch and called Harley over to me. *My poor girl.*

She enjoyed the sweet potato chews, so we always put a bunch in there, from the Easter Bunny.

"Liam, you pick your favorite, and Harley will eat hers with you, but just one for each of you," Paityn told him.

The rest of us did not have baskets. Even Ashton had stopped wanting one in the tenth grade. Mom just put out a cute, decorative tray, filled it with the green holiday grass, and then spread a variety of chocolates, peeps, and jelly beans on it for everyone to pick from all day long.

After breakfast, we rotated turns with the showers to get

ourselves presentable for the day, and then we hid some eggs while Liam was down for a short nap. Once they were all in their semi-obvious spots in the backyard, we waited for him to wake up and hunt. He got overly enthusiastic with each find, like he had discovered a massive treasure.

Elijah and Bethany arrived at the tail end to observe Liam cracking open each plastic egg, one by one, at the kitchen table.

"What do you have there, little guy?" Eli said as he took the chair next to Liam.

"Wook! I fine ess!" Liam exclaimed.

"Oh, eggs, you found eggs?" Eli rephrased his statement back to him.

Suddenly, I felt fingers running softly through my hair. I turned to see who was so gently trying to grasp my attention.

"Owen! You made it! It's so nice to see you!" I jumped to hug him with the warmest embrace that I had inside of me.

"I told you I wouldn't miss it, and I meant it." He flashed that gorgeous smile of his in my direction, which always made me melt.

"Thank you so much for being here. It means a lot to me." I held onto his hand tightly and tilted my head onto his broad shoulder.

"Of course! Has any news been shared yet?" He asked.

"Nope, not yet."

Minutes later, we took our seats at the dining room table, which Mom and I had set up with spring décor, and that was when it happened.

Just as we sat down, Bethany leaned over and whispered into Elijah's ear. He had an expression on his face that told me the news was quite a big deal.

"Can we get Oliver on Facetime?" Eli asked the whole room.

"It's not dinner time in California, so there's a chance he may not be available," Dad responded to Eli.

Dad stood up from the table to get his iPhone, while the rest of us looked at each other in suspense. He came back saying that he had Oli "on the line." I loved it so much that my dad still said that.

Dad sat down with his phone facing out toward the table but mostly pointed in the direction of where Elijah and Beth were sitting, patiently waiting to share their news.

"What is this? Dad was saying you have some big news, little brother?" Oliver did not waste any time.

"Well, as everyone knows, Bethany and I really want to have a family of our own," Eli led out.

It's happening!

"There has been some trouble in the past, and we have not been sure if having children was in the cards for us, but we continued to try," Bethany inserted.

The entire family had a pure look of optimistic anticipation on their faces.

"Bethany is pregnant again!" Elijah pronounced.

"Congratulations! This is so exciting! How far along are you?" The family simultaneously jumped over one another to express their delight.

"Almost four months, and we don't know the gender yet, but we should find out next month," Bethany answered.

Joy spread through the room instantly like wildfire.

It was just like Owen had said — this was a very bright light in the dark place the James family had been as of late.

CHAPTER TWENTY-FOUR

Journal Entry

*I*t's happening! Elijah and Bethany are having a baby! God, please look over all of them. My brother and his wife won't make it through another miscarriage.

This is huge for our family, with the devastation of losing Harley. We now have some hope in our lives, something to look forward to. What a welcomed surprise!

I can't wait to be an aunt again. Having a nephew has been such a blessing, and now I get to do it again. Is it wrong to want them to have a girl? Obviously, any healthy baby is more than enough, but it would be lovely to have a niece. I would spoil that little girl rotten. Who am I kidding? Whether it's a boy or girl, they are getting anything they want from Aunt Sophia. But I would like to be able to have nail painting parties and makeovers with a little princess.

My emotions are just all over the place. I have my growing relationship with Owen, and I have my lack of acceptance for what is going on with Harley, and now I have this wonderful news about Bethany being pregnant. All of that is a lot, but then add in what Ashton is struggling with. I don't even know which way is up.

CHAPTER TWENTY-FIVE

After Easter, an overpowering sense of loneliness overwhelmed me. Owen had returned to North Carolina, and I was planning my birthday weekend there with him, but that was still almost two weeks away. I needed to keep myself occupied to keep from obsessing over Harley, so I threw myself into my work. I handed out more business cards and updated my website. I was determined to stay very busy.

As I was uploading recent work from my camera memory card onto my laptop, a call came in. I expected it to be Owen telling me how much he misses me.

"Hello?" I answered, not even looking at the screen.

"Hi, Sophia, how are you?" inquired a deep voice on the end of the line.

Marcelo. The last time I spoke to him was the night that Rae and I ran into him at the lounge. I never reached out to him about doing that double date we had talked about, and he had not called or texted either.

"I'm doing okay, Marcelo. How are you these days?"

"I'm well. Thanks for asking. I know this is unexpected,

but I called you because I wanted to tell you about an event coming up this weekend for our work."

"Oh, really? My cousin, Ryan, hasn't mentioned it to me. What's it for?" I casually replied.

"It's the Spring Fling for our company. There is usually a decent cover band, and the food is always spectacular. If you don't have any plans yet for Saturday, maybe you and a few of your friends or family members would like to attend. Ryan said he was going to call your house anyway to tell you and your parents, so I figured I'd beat him to it."

"That was thoughtful of you. Let me talk to my parents and get back to you. I don't think I have a commitment for Saturday yet, but I'm also not sure if I can get my girlfriends to come with me with just a few days' notice."

"Sounds good. I'm sorry I didn't extend an invite sooner. I understand if you can't make it."

The vibe from the phone call was friendly, and it really didn't seem overly flirtatious like he was trying to snag a date with me. He works with my cousin, so I supposed it would be alright if I went, as long as I brought some other guests with me. My first instinct was to call Raelyn and see if she was available. At least, if I went there with Owen's sister, he would know that I was not attending with intentions of flirting or spending time with another guy.

The phone was already back in my hand.

"Hey, girl! What's up?" Rae answered after only the first ring.

"Hey, so I'm wondering if you have any plans for Saturday night. My cousin's work is hosting this Spring Fling thing. My parents are invited too, but I'm not sure if they are going. I could use the distraction." For some reason, I left out the part about Marcelo inviting me.

"Would Kevin be able to come too?"

"Yeah, that should be fine. I was told to bring a few people."

"Great! I'll talk to him about it when I see him. Should we invite Kendal? I haven't seen her in forever, and it would be nice for all of us to hang."

"That is a good idea. She called to check on me after I posted about Harley on Facebook and Instagram, but it's been a little while since I've connected with her."

"Get in touch with Kendal and give her the details, and I'll chat with you soon!" Rae said and then hung up the phone.

CHAPTER TWENTY-SIX

I found out later that my parents were declining the invite for Saturday evening, but Kendal accepted when I called her to tell her all about it, so she and I were meeting Raelyn and Kevin at their house so we could all drive together.

Kevin generously agreed to be the designated driver, which was awesome in more ways than one. Him driving obviously meant that us three girls could relax and have a fun time without worrying about being cautious with our alcohol intake, but it also meant that we got to ride in his brand-new cherry red Toyota Tundra truck. It had enough seating for five people and was equipped with surround sound and a panoramic sunroof. I always felt like a true country girl riding around in a big truck like that. Raelyn took shotgun, and Kendal and I hopped in the back.

When we pulled into the massive lot, there was plenty of parking, thankfully, because Kevin despised valet. I had to admit I wasn't a fan of it either. The idea of a stranger getting into my vehicle, moving and sitting in my driver seat, adjusting my mirrors, and parking it not so carefully near other cars soars way beyond my comfort level.

The four of us walked into the main lobby, where we found both my cousin and Marcelo sipping champagne and making small talk with guests near the entrance to the banquet room. Marcelo made eye contact with me and excused himself from conversation to greet us. *Please do not say you called.*

"Hello, Sophia! I am so glad you were able to make it. Hi, Raelyn, so good to see you. Is this your husband?" Marcelo was extremely polite and friendly, a guy most girls would fawn over and line up to go out with.

"Hey, there! Yes, I'm Kevin, Rae's better half," he snickered as he extended a hand. "Marcelo, this is my friend, Kendal. She's actually the reason I even know Raelyn." I nonchalantly pushed her in front of me.

"The pleasure is mine," Marcelo said as he shook her hand and glanced back at me. "All of you can call me Marc if you'd prefer, but I respond to Marcelo as well."

"I like Marcelo. It rolls so nicely off the tongue," Kendal replied with a playful lilt in her voice.

"I'll show you to a table and then help you with some beverages. Follow me this way!" Marcelo led us to a round table once we entered the luxurious banquet room.

A lovely young cocktail waitress was taking orders at the table next to ours, so we took our seats, assuming she would then come to us after she was finished with those guests. Kevin sat facing the stage where the band would be playing. Rae sat next to him, and then next to her was me, then Kendal on the end, leaving her a tad vulnerable to the possibility of a random loner filling the seat beside her.

After we placed our drink orders, I decided to go in search of my cousin and try to catch up with him on some family business. I wondered if the news about Elijah and Bethany expecting a baby in the upcoming months had spread to the extended parts of our family. I knew they hadn't announced anything officially on Facebook or other social media accounts just yet, but Mom or Dad may have said something to Aunt Capri. I found my cousin, Ryan, over by the appetizer tower piling some pigs in a blanket onto a small plate.

"Hey, save some for the rest of us. I'm starving!" I joked as I approached him with a quick hug and peck on the cheek. "How's it going?"

"Hey! It's going well. How are you?" Ryan continued lifting appetizer samples as he engaged in conversation. "Marc had mentioned he gave you a call."

"Yes, it was kind of both of you to think of us. I guess I'm as well as can be expected. Our whole family is pretty broken up about Harley, but we're trying our hardest to soak up the precious time we have left with her."

"My mom mentioned Harley being sick. I'm so sorry to hear about it. She's been such an amazing dog, Soph."

"Thank you for saying that. She really is extraordinary and completely irreplaceable. I don't know what I'll do without her."

"I should get over to see her soon. Are you home a lot on weekends or crazy busy with that photography career of yours?" Ryan asked. It was nice of him to inquire about my work, but for some reason, I was just not in the mood to talk about it at the moment.

"I am home sometimes on the weekends, but I won't be this next one. It's actually my birthday, so I am spending three days in North Carolina with Owen, Raelyn's brother."

"That's right! Happy Birthday! Wait, so are you and Owen dating?" He eyed me curiously.

"We are, yes," I told him. "He is in North Carolina for work for a few more weeks, and I promised him I would come for a visit." I realized that I was not calling Owen my boyfriend just yet, but that's because we had not had the exclusivity conversation. I feel like he knew I was not seeing anyone else, and I was sure he wasn't, but we still needed to have that talk.

"That's great! I'm really happy for you," Ryan replied. "I wonder if Marc knows you aren't available."

"I'm not really sure if he does, but to be honest, he hasn't shown much interest in me since we met," I shrugged it off.

"Really? He has definitely talked about you. However, he's also the type of guy who likes the woman to sort of make the first move as far as making plans to hang out romantically. At least, that's the vibe I get from him through the conversations we've had at work. It's probably why he has been having such a rough time getting back out there since his last relationship. I keep telling him he needs to initiate."

What my cousin was saying totally made sense and explained why he didn't call me after we met and why he then told me to text him about the double date.

"He'll find someone when he's ready, I'm sure," I said. "Oh, did you hear the latest James family news?"

"What news? Did something else happen?" Ryan asked.

"Bethany is pregnant! They just made the announcement on Easter, so I'm not sure how many people know." I thought it was fine that I told Ryan about it, considering Eli had mentioned that he was already telling some of his friends.

"What? That just made my night! I know how much they've wanted to have a child of their own and the hell they've gone through to try and get there."

"I can't imagine carrying a baby as long as Bethany did, growing so attached and connected, and then losing it. It was heart-wrenching."

"They deserve to have their happy ending, and I pray every day that they get it." Like me, Ryan always leaned on prayer when times got tough.

I nodded appreciatively. "I better get back to my table, but maybe I'll see you again before we leave." I realized my drink must have been delivered by this point, and I was afraid I was being quite rude to the guests I'd brought with me.

"Sophia, if I don't see you, send me a text soon to let me know when I can come over to see Harley."

"I surely will." I left Ryan and found a direct path back to the girls and Kevin.

I took my seat again between Rae and Kendal, and my timing was impeccable. Our cocktail waitress was just delivering our drinks and asking for our meal choices from the short list of options visible to us through a glass plated centerpiece, flowers protruding from the top. I settled on the steak and tilapia, otherwise known as the Surf and Turf, with creamy, garlic mashed potatoes and a heaping pile of steamed broccoli. Verbalizing my preference to the waitress made my mouth water and my stomach rumble audibly.

As we waited for our entrées, the cover band was doing a remarkable rendition of a Bob Marley classic. *Don't worry, about a thing. Every little thing, is gonna be alright. Singin' don't worry…* The relaxing tunes of a faraway island, along with my margarita on the rocks was lulling me into a state of relaxation. *This night could not have come at a better time.*

Everyone else had to have been feeling the exact same way, for in that moment, Raelyn leaned over and brought up what I had hoped to avoid.

"Sophia, we are having such a great time. It was really thoughtful of your cousin to invite all of us," Raelyn said ecstatically.

"Well, yeah, about that..." I started to come clean.

"About what? Did I get here just in time?" A deep male voice said behind me.

"Marcelo, hey, I didn't see you there." I froze right there in my tracks.

"No worries! Were you diving into some kind of gripping story?" he asked.

"Me? No, not all. I was just...well, I was going to comment on the band. They really are talented! Don't you agree?" I shifted awkwardly and gave Rae a side-eyed glance that inferred we would *talk more later,* as only best friends could do.

Marcelo seemed oblivious to the exchange. "Absolutely! We use them for all of our events. One of my coworkers is related to the lead singer, so they give us a fair deal. Do you mind if I join all of you for a drink?"

"Marcelo, you can sit over here next to me," Kendal offered.

Marcelo nodded graciously and pulled out the chair next to Kendal. "So, the three of you are close girlfriends, and Raelyn and Sophia met through Kendal? Do I have it right?"

"That's right! It turns out that nobody can resist Sophia's charm. My brother sure couldn't," Raelyn said, chuckling lightly.

"Your brother? Wait, what am I missing?" Marcelo asked.

Well, this was awkward. It would look shady for me to try to deflect, so there was no sense in me not shooting it straight.

"Raelyn's brother, Owen, and I recently started dating. He's a photographer just like me, and we get along very well." I barely looked in Marcelo's direction when I spoke, just in case he took any offense or was caught off guard by my words.

"Sounds like a perfect match then! That's great! Cheers!" Marcelo held up his tall glass full of beer, so everyone held up their drinks to clang glasses in celebration of the happy couple. I couldn't tell if the gesture was genuine or a cover for any hurt emotions my lack of transparency might have caused. *Ugh! I am going to need another drink.*

After that delightfully painful moment, Kevin made small talk with Marelo about the work they both did and where they went to college, while us girls did some people watching and some light-hearted gossiping about some of our small town nonsense. Once our meals arrived, Marcelo excused himself to join his coworkers at their table.

"Sophia, that guy Marc seems cool," Kevin said once Marcelo was out of earshot.

"That's what I said when we ran into him that night," Raelyn interjected. "If you weren't seeing Owen, I would still be pushing you to date Marc for sure."

"He is really cute!" Kendal chimed in. "He has his life together too, from what he was saying. How is he single?"

"I think he's fairly shy and needs an assertive woman to get the ball rolling." I didn't want to spill all of the information my cousin had just given me, but I felt it was okay to state my opinion based on what I was told.

A tiny smirk appeared on Kendal's face, as she tried to discreetly peek over at him a few yards away, and I could see the flicker of a smile pull at the corners of her mouth. *She likes him.*

CHAPTER TWENTY-SEVEN

"**E**xcuse me, sir! Can you help me find someone?" I leaned onto the counter at the service desk of the newly built resort in the Outer Banks.

"Sure, Miss. Give me the name, and I can ring their room," the gentleman replied from behind the desk.

"Well, the thing is I was hoping to surprise him. I wasn't supposed to arrive for another two hours, so he's not expecting me yet, and I want to show up at his door, cover the peephole, and catch him off guard. You understand, right?"

He looked at me wearily, like he was not sure how to respond.

"Ma'am, we have a confidentiality policy that prohibits me from giving out the room numbers of our guests. However, if you can prove you are a family member, I may be willing to bend the rules and have someone escort you to the floor."

"I can definitely give you proof of our relationship. His name is Owen Taylor. He's a photographer who's staying here to work for six weeks, and right here's a picture of me sitting with him from just two weeks ago in our hometown." I showed him the most recent selfie with Owen that we took over the Easter holiday at my house.

"You're in luck. I have spoken to Mr. Taylor on several occasions myself, and I remember him mentioning his excitement over your upcoming trip. He should be in there too, as I saw him return with his camera bag less than an hour ago." He took a minute, peered around the lobby for any watchful eyes, and then scrawled a number on a small slip of paper before handing it to me.

I thanked him and made my way toward the elevator to the left of the main lobby with the concierge. As I stepped in and pushed the button, I prayed that Owen was in his room and not out and about somewhere with the thought in his mind that I would not be flying into North Carolina for another couple of hours. *Please be up there.*

"Mr. Taylor's hotel room is right down this hall, last door on the right. Have a great stay!" The concierge pointed me to the room and then walked slowly back to the elevator, looking back once to check on me.

Owen's room was on the fourth floor of the resort, and I remembered from our conversations that he had mentioned a nice view of the ocean. I couldn't wait to get into his room and see his face. *Oh, how I miss that face.*

I knocked twice on the door and covered the peephole.

"One moment please. Who's there?" Owen softly shouted from the inside of his suite.

I stayed silent, so I wouldn't blow my cover.

"Hello? Is someone out there? Who is it?" he asked again.

I knocked on the door another time, but I still kept quiet. He fumbled with the doorknob for a few seconds and then swung the door open suspiciously.

Before he could utter a word of frustration for the person on the other side not announcing themselves, I shouted out.

"Surprise! I'm here early!" I held out my arms to welcome a big hug from Owen, and instead, he lifted me up off of the ground and pulled my legs up around him. Our bodies were so tightly wrapped together that I could hear and feel how fast his heart was beating with excitement.

"Sophia! Wow! I was just about to shower and get dressed so I could pick something up that I ordered for you and then go to meet you at the airport, but I'm so happy you're here already! Oh my God, I love you!" The words flew out of his mouth so fast I wasn't sure how to react. I stared at him, at his eyes, at his mouth, at him standing there with his hands sitting gently at the center of my back. I stared longer. He kissed me and then placed his forehead up against mine, looking into my eyes. *Tell him, you idiot.*

"I love you too, Owen. I always have." There was no taking it back, and I wouldn't even if I could.

"You might need to show me how much." He grabbed one of my bags, ushered me inside of his room, and then shut the door behind me, slipping one of those 'do not disturb' signs on the outside knob.

We barely made it ten feet into the room before he began undressing, while intensely gazing at me from head to toe.

I kicked my shoes off and asked playfully, "Are you taking that shower you mentioned before?"

"I plan to, but I was thinking maybe you could join me." He slipped out of every inch of clothing he was wearing until he was completely and beautifully naked, and then offered to help remove all of mine.

I was finding it hard to help him, as I could not divert my eyes from his masterpiece of a body. Owen was not just a pretty face. He took care of himself very well, always watching what he ate and hitting the gym three to four times a week. If I had to pick a favorite part of his physical appearance, I would probably say his super toned arms. Although, his chest and abs were certainly a close second, and the view was just as nice as you moved to his south end too. Never had I before seen more muscular and perfectly sculpted calves on a person, unless of course if you counted professional soccer players.

I managed to regain focus long enough to enjoy the two of us working together to make sure I matched his state of undress. Owen took my hand and led me to his bathroom, where I noticed the sliding door shower with a rainfall head.

As he stepped onto the tile floor and turned on the faucet, I immediately followed closely behind to have both of my arms wrapped around the front of him. The hot water poured over us, slowly dripping down our skin. Several minutes passed like seconds. I lathered him with body wash as if he had been covered in mud and took my time rinsing all of it off. Owen pinned me to the shower wall, and years of fantasies that have been played and replayed in my mind became a reality exceeding every expectation.

After our shower concluded, we put ourselves together to look as presentable as possible, even though I was so relaxed I could have fallen asleep with Owen right then in his king size bed — the one I knew would undoubtedly get much use over the weekend.

Owen told me he wanted to show me the entire resort and the breathtaking landscape surrounding it, so we both slid into our most comfortable walking shoes and began our journey. I was so excited to see every little spot where he had been conducting his work since he arrived in North Carolina.

As we traveled around, Owen described each shoot in detail to help me create the image in my mind of the occasion where he photographed various individuals, couples, and both small and large groups who were celebrating engagements, weddings, anniversary parties, birthday parties, and galas.

"What would you say has been your favorite event you've worked while being here?" I asked him.

"Hmm...that's a good question. I think I'm going to have to say the wedding that took place here last weekend. I was able to get a ton of both posed and candid shots of the happy couple and all of their family and guests celebrating the unity of two people who were clearly head over heels in love with each other. It was so refreshing to see and almost brought out my inner mush."

"Are you saying you almost cried?" I tickled him a little as I asked, making sure he knew I thought it was absolutely adorable if he had wept a little.

"I did not cry, but my eyes did well up once or twice. They had the kind of relationship I hope to have with my wife one day." Owen took his eyes off of the path in front of us and locked eyes with me.

I tried to speak past the lump in my throat. "That's really sweet. Thank you for sharing that with me." I folded my fingers around his hand as we continued walking around the resort.

"Let's grab some food, and then we can do a nightcap on my terrace. It's small, but it does have a partial view of the beach and the ocean, and I have some wine in the room."

"You know how much I love the beach and my wine." I praised him for his attentiveness.

We went into a pizza shop inside the resort and picked up some food to bring back to the room. Since it was a warm night in April, Owen set us up on the balcony at a small black steel table. He opened a large bottle of cabernet and administered two very heavy pours.

"To you and to your birthday!" he said as he raised his

wine glass.

"I will cheers to that," I said with a light chuckle and tipped my glass to his.

"I'm honored that you chose to spend your birthday weekend with me, you know. I hope your family didn't mind a whole lot that I stole you away."

"Well, they understood that I wanted to be with you, so they didn't give me too much of a hard time. I'll celebrate with them another day."

We ate our tomato pie, and we drank our wine, and we reminisced about the many times we have spent together over the years not thinking the other had even the tiniest bit of interest in more than a friendship. Before we knew it, it was past midnight.

"Sophia, guess what?" Owen asked while pulling my chair closer to his.

"What is that?" I replied, fitting my arm into the open space between his arm and his chair.

"Happy Birthday!" He said to me and then leaned in to kiss my cheek, making me smile.

"Oh, you're right!" I looked at my watch on my right hand to see that it was in fact two minutes into my birthday. I had lost all track of time while entranced in deep conversation that could quite possibly continue for hours, if not days, if we'd let it. He was the easiest and most comfortable person to talk to. "Thank you!"

"Guess what else?" Owen reached to put his right arm around to my right side so that we were as snuggled up as we could be while sitting in separate chairs.

"What else?" I said, putting my head on his right shoulder from the side.

"I want you to be my girlfriend, all mine. Is that something...you might be interested in?"

I took a deep breath in and out and then took his left cheek with my right hand to bring his face toward me. I softly kissed his lips with my eyes open, knowing his would be open too.

"Owen, that is exactly what I am interested in." I told him, my face still inches from his.

We kissed some more, stopping randomly to look at each other and smile at this new development in our relationship. We eventually ventured back indoors and to the bed, where we slept with our bodies intertwined. It was one of the best night's sleep I had in a while, for the time we were sleeping anyway.

The next two days were pure bliss, as we took a romantic walk on the beach and had a long soak in the outside hot tub by the pool. We also sipped champagne to toast my birthday and laughed hysterically and loudly at the comedy show Owen had surprised me with. There were roses and chocolate cake, and there was room service to provide us with breakfast in bed on my last day there. I would not change one single moment of the weekend. I would only change having to leave him at all.

"It won't be much longer," Owen said, pressing a kiss to my head as we said goodbye in front of the airport late Sunday afternoon.

"I know." I nuzzled deeply into his chest. "This job will be finished, and you will be back home soon. I am just going to miss you, a lot." I held on tighter, not daring to let go first.

"Send me a text when you land, and we'll chat later when you get back home to your house," he said.

"I will. I promise." I hugged him and reminded him to be safe and to think of me often. I walked away, turning around once to wave and blow him one last kiss.

"I love you, Sophia," he yelled to me.
"I love you right back."

CHAPTER TWENTY-EIGHT

Journal Entry

I 'm in love. Like actually and fully in love. I've always been interested, and I've always cared, even enough to say that I loved him as a person and as a good friend, but it's more now. It's a lot more. I'm completely in love with Owen.

I guess I never thought I would even have the chance to explore it, so I protected myself from getting there emotionally. The last time I was in a relationship, I let my guard down, and I got hurt. And I wasn't even in love that time. I thought I was at first, but by the end, I realized that I was just crazy about the idea of it all.

God, don't let me be wrong this time. Please let me know myself now. I've taken time to think about what I want for my life and the kind of person I want to share it with. I've also thought about what I don't want, which is just as important. Growth comes from experiences and reflection. And I reflect on everything. Maybe sometimes too much. But I'm a lot better than I was before I got help.

Once I realized there was a problem, I was able to work on solutions. Nothing in your life changes if you don't change — and I'm so glad to say that I've changed.

CHAPTER TWENTY-NINE

While I was at the airport, I received two phone calls, which I didn't answer because I was going through security and then waiting to board my flight. Both made me wonder, but I decided not to waste too much time hypothesizing while on the plane.

One call had been from Paityn, who I had just briefly spoken to the day before when she called to wish me a happy birthday, so I was uncertain why she'd be calling again so soon. The other was someone who I really thought I wouldn't hear from again, especially after the last time I saw him. *Why is Marcelo calling me? What could he possibly have to say?*

When I reached my front porch, I checked my watch to see if it would be too late to give Paityn a ring back. I had already decided I wouldn't call Marcelo back. He was well aware I was with Owen, and it was official after the weekend we just had, so I felt it would be best not to give Marcelo the wrong idea.

"Hello?" Paityn said on the other end after two rings.

"Paityn, hey, I saw you called. Sorry I didn't answer. I just got home from my visit with Owen."

"No problem. I didn't think yesterday was a good time to tell you about this, and I was actually going to wait a few more days to reach out, but I have been unable to get it off my mind all day," Paityn said cryptically.

"What is it? Did something happen? Are you okay?" I asked her frantically.

"We're all fine. I just know you've been concerned with how Liam is developing as a toddler, and I promised I would give you a full report after we had him evaluated." She sounded fairly calm, so I assumed it couldn't be too bad.

"Well, go ahead," I urged.

"His pediatrician had a specialist conduct testing to see if and why there were any cognitive delays, and we were honestly worried that he might be on the autism spectrum, even though we can surely handle that."

"Okay, and what did the results show?" I asked as patiently as I possibly could.

"We found out that along with having a delay in vocabulary, Liam has a receptive and expressive language disorder. This means he not only struggles to get his meaning or message across to other people, but he struggles to understand and process messages and information that others are trying to communicate to him," Paityn explained to me.

"Paityn, this makes so much sense. I am so glad you and Bradley know what Liam is facing now. Do you have information on how to help him improve? What kind of services will he need?"

"The plan is to have Liam start working with a speech and language therapist once a week. If we feel like he needs more sessions, they will see him twice a week."

"That sounds great! I appreciate you updating me, and I'm

relieved that you have answers and a plan of action." I gave a big sigh, for both myself and her. "Early intervention is key."

The next afternoon while I was getting ready for a shoot, my phone vibrated on the end table. I looked to see I had one new message.

Marcelo wrote and asked for me to call him when I had the chance. For the life of me, I could not figure out why he'd be calling me. He didn't call after we first met, and he didn't call after Rae and I ran into him while we were out.

I decided to type back to him that I was leaving the house soon to go to a job and didn't have time to talk. He immediately responded by saying he had a question for me about someone I know and that he would appreciate it if I could call him after work. *Who is he talking about?*

I agreed, and I put it out of my mind. The location of the shoot was about thirty minutes away, and I knew I had to be on my game. I was shooting a spread for prom season, and there were over twenty young women modeling this year's gowns. *Where were these dramatic and glamorous dresses when I was in high school?*

I photographed low cut, high slit, two piece, short and long, form-fitting, strapless, and open back ensembles. The most popular trend seemed to be nude fabric placed between the dress' material to make it appear as if you are showing skin from a distance. As my camera flashed, I was picturing myself in New York during Fashion Week at the end of the runway being one of the most sought-after photographers to work the event and loving every millisecond. I had to make a name for myself, and I was not stopping until I did.

When I packed up to go home, I saw another text on my phone, but this time it was not Marcelo, it was Ashton, telling me he needed my advice. I really hoped that when he went off to college in Tennessee come August, he would still reach out for my help. It was nice to feel needed by my baby brother, who was not such a baby anymore.

I sent Ashton a text back to let him know I was on my way home, and that it made much more sense to speak in person. He said he'd be home, so I decided I might as well call Marcelo to see what had his knickers in such a twist. The phone rang once before he picked up, as if he had been holding the cell in his hand awaiting my call.

"Sophia! Thank you so much for getting back to me," Marcelo said, his voice full of gratitude.

"Well, it seemed really important, so I thought better of leaving you hanging for a while. Is everything okay?" I asked him, hoping he did not have a serious concern.

"Everything is fine. I just want to talk to you about something. Do you have a few minutes?" Marcelo's tone was very calm and casual, but I still could not imagine what he needed to talk to me about. Him and I were more like acquaintances than friends, and he knew I was dating Owen.

"I have some time, yes. What's this about?"

"I hope you don't think this is weird, but..."

"Wait, Marcelo! Let me interject for a second. You know I have a boyfriend now, right?"

"Yes, I remember. You are with your friend, Raelyn's brother, right?"

"That's correct. I just wanted to make sure we were on the same page. Okay now, go ahead with what you were saying." I almost felt bad at this point for interrupting and making assumptions, especially because it didn't appear he wanted to date me. I was puzzled.

"Well, I have been thinking...I'm just wondering...you

know your friend, the one you brought with you to the Spring Fling, the nice one with the pretty dark hair?"

"You mean Kendal?"

"Yes, Kendal. Do...do you know if she's currently seeing anyone? Do you mind that I'm asking?" He was respectful and awkward at the same time, and it surprised me that he was being assertive enough to ask me about her after what my cousin had told me.

"As far as I know, she's single. This is what you wanted to talk to me about? You like Kendal?" I hope I did not come off as jealous because I wasn't at all. I was more astonished than anything. Kendal was a catch, but it wasn't every day that a guy you almost went out with calls you to ask about your friend.

"Do you think she would be alright with you giving me her number? I would like to see her again. Did she say anything to you about me that night or since then?" Marcelo was fishing, but I wasn't saying too much, even though I did notice Kendal taking a liking to him.

"She may have mentioned you being nice and possibly good-looking or something of that nature while we were at the table. I do not remember the details, Marcelo."

"I felt a cool vibe between us, Sophia. What do you think?"

"How about I send her a text to ask her if I can pass along her contact information, and I will send it to you if she says it's alright?"

"That works for me. Thank you for your help!"

We hung up, and I pulled into our driveway. I sent the message like I promised, still wondering what gave Marcelo the courage to act on his interest for Kendal. It wasn't like he was suggesting a group event like how he called to invite me to the Spring Fling and told me to bring others. *Maybe he's not so shy if he feels like it's something he really wants. Either that, or he decided to take my cousin's advice about being the one to initiate a date.*

I had to go find Ashton. Secretly, I was wishing for him to be seeking my advice about Riley. They were so close and had such a strong friendship, and they were moving to the same city for school to attend the same university. They had to get over the hurdle that had been created.

I checked on Harley, who was sound asleep in her bed in the family room with my mom passed out on the couch next to her. Ashton was missing from the downstairs scene, so I figured he had to be in his room. I rapidly climbed the steps to see a light beaming out of his partially open doorway, and I knocked twice as I watched him scrolling on his desktop.

"Soph! Hey! Come on in; I want to get your opinion." He welcomed me, still staring at the screen. This sounded good.

"Lay it on me, Ash! What's going on?"

"The senior prom is coming up soon. I need you to help me with my prom-posal. Can you?"

"Sure! Are you searching online for ideas? Have you narrowed it down?"

"I found a few popular ones, but I was thinking of tweaking it to better fit my date." Ashton was overly enthusiastic for the very first time this entire school year.

"What is his favorite movie, Ash?"

"Whose favorite movie?" He asked me with a bewildered expression on his face.

"The person you want to ask...what is he into? Or she! Sorry! Do they have a favorite movie or song that you can use as a guide?"

"Why did you assume I would want to ask a guy? Do you think I want everyone to think I'm gay or bisexual?"

"I am so sorry, Ash! I didn't mean to offend you or jump to conclusions. Don't be upset with me."

"I am not upset. It's just that nobody knows about me being into both guys and girls; I have not even told Mom and Dad yet, and I do not know how I am going to. I feel like there is no way that they will ever understand."

"Mom and Dad are great! They raised all of us to be accepting of any differences a person may have. You are their son, and they will love you no matter what!" I tried to assure him he had nothing to worry about.

"I know you're right, and I do know that I have to tell them eventually, but I'm not ready. I'm just not there yet."

"I get it, completely. Tell me more about this girl then. Give me the tea!" I attempted to match the lingo his generation was currently using, but my delivery was not the best.

"Soph, stop!" Ashton said with laughter and a side smirk.

"Who is she, buddy? Do you have class with her?"

"I do have class with her. I didn't really talk to her much until after the winter break, and we only chat here and there when there is downtime in class or if we get put into a group together for an activity. She is so chill and so pretty, and I feel like she would be a lot of fun to go with."

"That is so exciting! What's her name?" I was so curious.

"Her name is Faith. She has black hair, usually in braids or curls, dark skin, and she is a couple of inches shorter than me." Ashton began to describe his potential date, but I needed a visual.

"I love her name! Do you have a picture?"

He typed on his keyboard to load the high school webpage, where he clicked on photos of this year's seniors until he got to her. *Wow!*

"Here she is! This is Faith. She's super cool! Do you think she'll say yes to going with me?" he asked, lacking confidence.

"Great taste, Ashton! Of course, she will. Why wouldn't she want to go with a nice guy like you?"

"Thanks! I'm nervous, but I cannot wait to ask her."

"Let's discuss the way you will do it. Do you want to do it at school or away from school?"

"I have narrowed it down to three options, two of which would be away from the school building, but one I thought of would be in the class that we have together. If I pick the one at school, I may need help from the teacher."

"What do the three options entail? I will help you decide!" I told him excitedly. I honestly could not wait to hear what he had already come up with.

"The first one is finding out what her favorite song is and changing the words to ask her to go with me to the prom. The second option is asking her to go over to the park with me over the weekend and spelling out prom and a question mark with giant rocks. Finally, the third option would be in our class at school, during the warm-up we do each day. The teacher always projects the daily warm-up onto the white board and goes over the agenda, so I am thinking of having her type out what I want to say on the top of the agenda."

"I like all three of them, but I do have a question. What will you do after your teacher shows the class the promposal?"

"After Faith sees it, I am going to pull out a red silk rose from my backpack and stand up to face her while holding it out. What do you think?" His face lit up.

"Ashton, I love it. I think she will love it too." *What girl would say no to that proposition?* "Really nice job!

"Thanks! Just don't get your hopes up yet," he said.

I gave him more encouragement about how fortunate she would be to go with him, and I left him to his planning.

CHAPTER THIRTY

The next morning, I woke up to see on my phone that Kendal had texted me back. She gave me the go-ahead to give Marcelo her number. I really wasn't all that surprised since she was checking him out that first night they met. Some people would be jealous if a guy or woman they were potentially going to date started showing interest in their friend, but I was too happy with Owen to even care. I actually gave Kendal my blessing and told her to go for it. Marcelo seemed like a great guy, and she deserved nothing but the best.

After forwarding her number to Marcelo, I decided to spend the day with Harley. I lived in constant fear that her condition could worsen at any time. I planned to smother her with affection until the moment came when I'd have to say goodbye. She had slept in my bed right next to me every single night since she was a puppy, and I now had to mentally prepare myself for when I would have to go to sleep without her. My chest tightened, and my throat constricted, threatening a fresh wave of tears.

I'll never make it through this.

Harley was laying on the couch when I came to get her to put her carnation pink harness on. She was so good about wearing it and always got all riled up when she saw any of us approaching her with it. This time, though still excited, she lacked her usual bounce and fervor, a clear indication of how weak she was becoming. My prayers had not brought her a miraculous recovery yet, but they may have been giving us some more time with our girl.

"Come on, girl! Want to go for a walk?"

Her tail wagged as I strapped her in and fastened the leash. Once we were outdoors in the fresh spring air, my mood lifted. I remembered how much Harley enjoyed stopping to literally smell the roses in the bushes along the path we chose to frequent for our walks. Flashes of her rolling around in newly cut grass sprung to my mind. She loved the way it felt on her back and would flop back and forth with a huge grin on her face from ear to ear, tail wagging every which way. The memories filled my heart with pure joy, and I stopped to pet her head in appreciation.

Harley walked a bit slower these days, which at first made everyone in the James family sad, but then we realized we were grateful she was still getting around without any help. I liked to find the positive side in every situation, and this wasn't any different. Though it wasn't easy to always look on the bright side, it oddly offered me a feeling of control when things were most difficult. I couldn't control the situation or the circumstances, but I could control the way I thought about it and learned from it.

After our walk, which was not as lengthy as it had been many times in the past, Harley and I cuddled up in the sunroom on the couch, and I turned on a USA women's soccer game. She really enjoyed watching just as much as I did. Every time I shouted at the television, Harley popped up to give a little howl. We watched the whole game and then both dozed off once it concluded. It was only when I heard my mom's voice urging me with fear to wake up that I realized three hours had gone by.

Half out of it, I sat up, my girl still very close. Mom had tears in her eyes. *What is going on?*

"Mom, what happened? Are you okay?" I asked her while hugging Harley for comfort.

"Honey, we have to go. Can you pull yourself together fast?" She was gathering a variety of items into her purse.

"Where are we going? What happened, Mom?"

"It's Bethany! She's at the hospital. There was a fall."

Was it the stairs? Did she trip? All I could think about was the bad luck that seemed to follow my brother and Bethany.

It'll be okay. It'll be okay.

My mom continued, her voice interrupting the mantra coursing through my brain. "It was the stairs. She was bringing laundry down from the bedroom in a basket, and she lost her footing. Elijah picked her up and rushed her to the hospital."

"Give me two minutes, Mom. I'll meet you at the car."

"I'll go start it up. Your dad and Ashton will meet us there as soon as they can leave work," Mom said, heading outside.

Harley looked so confused, but I hugged her one more time and gave her a treat before I ran out the door. On the drive to the hospital, Mom and I didn't say much. Worry filled us to the point of being speechless, as the worst possible outcomes ran through our minds.

Please God, do not let them lose the baby.

———

Elijah met us and took us to the waiting area nearest to her room. He quickly but carefully explained how their doctor was still evaluating Bethany and the baby but that they should have some answers soon. At this point, she was just over four months along, and I needed to pray that the fall didn't cause any complications.

"Eli, can you point me in the direction of the chapel? I want to go light a candle and say some prayers for Beth and the baby."

"I'll walk you. Bethany's parents are in there already, so I can bring them back with me if they are through," he replied.

I gave my brother a big hug and assured him we were all there for them. I had no idea how he would ever recover from another miscarriage.

We opened the door to the hospital chapel to see both of her parents lighting candles in front of a remarkable stained glass window illuminated with the day's bright sun. Elijah approached them and proceeded to light one himself.

"Sophia, I'm going to take them back with me. Can you find your way back alright?"

"Yes, I'll be fine. Thank you. I'm so sorry this happened," I said to all of them. "Stay strong."

They left me alone to pray, and I said every prayer I could think of, along with some I came up with at the moment. I lit a candle and then thought I should call Owen to give him a heads up to what was going on. Thankfully, I caught him at a decent time, and he sent his good vibes to all of us. I really wished he were with us right then. I knew just seeing him and giving him a hug would make me feel so much better.

———

Walking back to the waiting area outside of Bethany's hospital room, all I could think about was how the James family could not handle any more grief. With everything going on with Harley, and with Ashton struggling so much over this school year, the last thing we needed was another tragedy. Positivity went a long way though, so I had to put on a brave face for my brother and give him all of the support I could.

"Any news?" I said as I reached the group. *Please let there be an update.*

No sooner did I get the words out did Bethany's doctor come walking up to us, her demeanor calm and upbeat. "Good news! Both mom and baby are stable. The heartbeat is still very strong. We are going to keep them here overnight for monitoring, and I will allow visitors in just a few moments."

"Thank God!" Elijah released a deep breath. "So, there were no injuries or anything to my wife or the baby? The fall didn't hurt them?"

"You married a fighter, son, and it looks like that daughter of yours will take after her mom," the doctor said.

"Wait! What? Did you...hold on..." He was trying to catch his breath and make sure he was not hearing things. "Did you say I'm having a daughter? It's a girl? Oh my!" He turned to address the rest of us, like we had been hanging on the doctor's every word. "Was everyone listening? Did everyone hear that? I'm having a girl!" Elijah was bursting with excitement. I too could barely contain myself.

"Eli! That's amazing! I'm going to have a niece!" I hugged him again and then circled around to hug everyone else in the room. Elijah did the same and then darted away to be with Beth. *Truth be told, I'd been hoping for a girl all along.*

Dad and Ashton arrived approximately fifteen minutes after we heard the news, and they were just as ecstatic as the rest of us. My parents sat there for about a half an hour thinking of family names from the past that they could suggest to Elijah for their baby girl, knowing it may not matter anyway, since my brother and Bethany probably had a ton of names already picked out from even before they had miscarried. It was kind of nice to hypothesize possible outcomes for the first and middle name though. I was such a sucker for that stuff.

After I sent Owen, Rae, and Kendal a text to tell them I was going to be an aunt to my first niece, the lot of us strolled down to the room to check on Mom and baby and congratulate them as a family for the incredible new discovery.

"Beth, how do you feel about finding out it is a girl? Did you want to know? Were you planning to find out? Did you have an inkling?" The questions poured out of my mouth like word vomit.

"Whoa, Sophia!" Bethany said while laughing. "Let's see... I'm over the moon to find out it is a girl. And as much as we would have loved to be surprised, both of us wanted to know in a way. I did have a feeling that it might be a girl, and to be honest, I was kind of hoping it was," she said as her eyes scanned the room and landed on my brother.

Eli stepped in to continue, "We were still on the fence about whether or not we wanted to find out the gender, so though this has definitely caught us off guard, I'd have to agree I'm beyond delighted," Elijah said with strong emotion.

"I'm so happy for both of you." I stood up from my chair where I sat near the side of the hospital bed to give Bethany's hand a tight squeeze.

"Thank you! All of you — for being here for us and for your prayers and kind words. We will be keeping you updated until this little bundle of joy makes her debut!" Elijah's eyes twinkled with gratitude.

"Sweetheart, any ideas of when exactly that might be? Your father and I came up with some names this evening," Mom half-jokingly said as she nudged my dad.

"The baby is due on September 25, so it's going to be a nervous five months for us," Bethany told us.

"Well, we'll let you have some alone time," Dad replied as

he made his way to the door. "Get some rest, and we'll call and check in on you tomorrow."

Her parents said their goodbyes as well, and we filed out to the parking lot together. We wished them a safe ride home before hopping into our cars to head home, where I planned to resume my snuggles with Harley.

CHAPTER THIRTY-ONE

"Sophia! Sophia! Where are you? I have news! Sophia!" Ashton bellowed through the house.

"Ashton? Ash! I'm up here giving Harley a bath." I opened the bathroom door to shout down to him down the hallway, uncertain if he could hear me.

I heard footsteps approaching the top of the landing, and I quickly checked my watch before Ashton found me. I didn't want him to think I was too busy to hear his news. Thankfully, I had just enough time to hear the story and dry Harley off before I had to leave for work.

"Sophia! Guess what?" Ashton said as he rushed into the bathroom with a humongous smile splattered across his face.

"How many guesses do I get?" I playfully responded.

"I'll give you two guesses, but if you don't get it after that, I'm spilling the tea!" I loved how the word 'tea' had taken on a new meaning of the fresh gossip in our current day.

"My first guess is that you changed your mind about going so far away to college. Am I right? You're going to stay closer instead? Please say that you are."

"Nope. Incorrect. Sorry, Soph. I'm still going to Nashville

for college, and I cannot wait!" he said, raising his voice. "Guess again!"

"Bummer, buddy! Well, you had better let me take you to Tennessee when it's time to move you in. I've never been to Nashville, but I hear it's a blast."

"I promise you can come with Mom and Dad to take me to school in August. Does that make you feel better?"

"Yes, actually, it does. Maybe I'll make it a girls trip and bring Rae and Kendal with me!"

"That would be fun. But you're getting off topic! Guess again!" he urged.

"My second guess is that maybe, just maybe, you have yourself a prom

date? Is that it?" I toyed with him.

"Yes! I asked her, and she agreed to go with me! I'm so stoked. Can you

tell?"

"It's very obvious how hyped up you are. That's great! Tell me everything. Do not leave out any details. Go!"

"First, you should know that I had to go to Ms. Pearson at school. I needed her to help me project onto the white board, and I also didn't want her thinking I was randomly disrupting class."

"Alright, I'm with you. You convinced your World Literature teacher to assist you. Continue..." I gestured with a rolling hand and my eyes wide in suspense.

"I followed the plan I brainstormed with you about having the question show up for her in the daily announcements on our agenda. My teacher read our lesson objective and our warm-up assignment, and then she went through our agenda. Just when the class thought she was going to close out of the screen on the board with her smartboard remote, another screen popped up with bolded capital letters typed out. It read: "IF I HAVE FAITH, I HAVE ALL I NEED.""

"Ashton! I love that! Did you think of that? What happened next?"

"I did think of it! Everyone in the class looked at the board in confusion, and our teacher's eyes kept bouncing between Faith and me. I pulled the silk rose out of my backpack and then stood up to face her. At that moment, she knew something was about to happen, and the rest of the kids started to catch on too. I looked at her face and held the rose out to her. She smiled, while blushing, and stood up. And then I just...asked. She took the rose and hugged me, and I was immediately congratulated by a wild round of applause, echoing from all sides. I gave her a hug and sat back down, just soaking in the most exhilarating moment that I have had all school year."

"That is the sweetest story I've heard in a long time. I can see how happy this is making you, and I'm so happy for you too. Have you told Mom and Dad yet?" I knew they'd be ecstatic for Ashton.

"You are the first person I told, but I'm planning to tell them later. I'm sure Mom will be grabbing for her camera minutes after I share the news so she can document the way my face looked on the day I asked someone to the prom!" Ashton laughed, and I laughed with him, knowing how completely accurate that was.

"Facts!" I replied, with a little sneer on my face.

He held up a hand in protest. "Stop, Sophia, just stop. You will never pull off my generation's slang."

Ashton had intentions of telling Mom and Dad together when Dad got home from work that evening. He said he refused to repeat the story two more times, and I kind of couldn't blame him. I knew they'd be just as thrilled for him as I was, and maybe after the prom, he could finally open up to them about him being bisexual.

In the meantime, I was mentally and emotionally preparing myself to be reunited with Owen, who was *finally* coming home after his long work adventure. On one hand, it felt like he had just left and that these past six weeks flew by; on the other hand, I had missed him so much that it felt like it'd been a lifetime without him. Thank goodness he was going to be around because I did not think I could handle going through the rest of Harley's illness alone. Of course, I had my family, but it was a different type of support with Owen. I was counting down the minutes until he got back. *Why don't we have the ability to fast-forward time when we need to?*

The doorbell rang, and I swiftly glided down the stairs as if I was riding on a magic carpet. His beautiful eyes and smile flashed through my mind as I made my way to the foyer and reached for the doorknob.

"Owen, it's you! Get over here!" I held out my arms to give him the biggest hug in the world. He moved in for my embrace, and I felt true comfort for the first time since I'd left him at the resort.

"It is so good to see you. I needed this!" Owen said as his body was still closely against mine. "How are you?"

"Better now that you're home! I feel like I can breathe again, baby." He had no idea how good he made me feel. "Tell me more about your last week."

"Would you want to go and grab a bite with me? I can tell you all about it once we get there." Owen asked, and I was so grateful because I was famished.

"Yes! I'm so hungry. Let me get my purse, and we can go."

We decided on a little Chinese restaurant just a few minutes down the road from my house. Owen ordered the sesame chicken with pork fried rice, and I ordered the chicken and broccoli with pork fried rice, and we threw in some wonton soup as well. This place was the best in the area, right down to their fresh fortune cookies and their green tea. I usually did not like egg rolls, but I *always* ate them there.

I was excited to hear about Owen's last week in North Carolina, but secretly, I hoped it didn't go so spectacularly that he would be asked to go back again any time soon. I needed him home so we could give this a real chance to see where it was headed.

Once our drinks and soup arrived, Owen began to tell me about a sixteenth birthday party that took place a few days before he left and another rehearsal dinner, both of which were held in the smaller banquet room at the resort. He told me stories of the cool shots he arranged of the families and friend groups. As I listened to him share the details enthusiastically, an idea sprang to mind. Owen spent the last six weeks away on location working a huge variety of events, making a name for himself, doing exactly what I wanted to be doing, although I also wanted to travel outside of our country from time to time.

An idea started to take form in my mind, and before I could stop myself, I asked, "Owen, can I maybe run something by you?"

He took a sip from his drink and said, "Of course! What's on your mind?"

"Have you ever thought about working with a partner, sort of like how we collaborated in the Poconos and other occasions for the magazine?" I knew he would have liked to have a business where he did not have to report to anyone, just like I did, but I wondered if he wanted to do that on his own or if he'd ever considered being half of something bigger.

"I honestly have never envisioned having a partner for my future work, but lately it has occurred to me how being on a solid team could be extremely beneficial." I wasn't quite sure if he was only talking about the business anymore. He continued, "There were a few situations over the last six weeks where having two of us would have enhanced the photoshoot immensely. For example, two people could spread out at a social or formal event and take double the amount of candid shots of the guests than one person can." Owen's good point gave me the courage to continue.

"Yes, exactly. Two heads, or sets of eyes, are better than one in many areas of this profession. I would love to have a partner, if it were someone I admired and respected. I would obviously have to get along with them well and have a similar work ethic." I stopped to see if there was anything else he wanted to add.

"Sophia, I love where you're going with this, and I really do see potential in the whole idea, but is this crazy? Too soon? I mean, I know we have a lot in common and can accept feedback from each other graciously, but do you think that we could be successful for the long haul professionally? Do you think that it puts too much pressure on our new relationship?"

I was relieved to hear him seriously considering the proposal. I couldn't argue his points — they were valid, and the prospect of messing it all up was beyond terrifying. However, the alternative was almost too good to pass up. Not only would Owen and I get to share all of our talents and perspectives, figuratively and quite literally, but us being a team would mean that we would not have to leave each other for extended periods of time and risk having it jeopardize the closeness of our growing relationship.

"I actually do think we would work well as a team, and I think our personal and professional connection would provide us with the potential for excellent longevity. Does it have the possibility of crashing and burning? Sure it does, but don't you think that something like this, like us, is worth the risk?" I prayed hard that he would have an open mind and a positive outlook.

"Of course, we're worth the risk. And I would never pick just anyone to partner with. It would have to be someone I value, trust, and feel comfortable with, as well as someone with whom I had the utmost respect and confidence."

"Well, clearly all of those things are vital for a strong partnership. I could not agree with you more." I stared at his face impatiently, trying to read him and wanting to pull the words from his mouth, in the effort of not dancing around it any longer.

Just say it. Just say what you want. "First, I need to get your opinion on something. Okay?" *Oh no...is he trying to change the subject?* We were just about at the finish line of this discussion, mere inches away, and now he wanted to hear my thoughts on something. I cleared my throat and sipped my water, trying to swallow against the dryness of my mouth. "I'm all ears," I said, my voice dripping with reluctance.

"How does the name 'Taylor James' sound for a company name?" Owen asked with that sexy voice he killed me with.

"Wait, what are you saying?" I could feel the knots in my stomach beginning to untangle. I knew what he was saying, but I needed him to say it explicitly.

"I think you know," he said, as his eyebrows lifted playfully. "What if we join forces and start a photography business together? What do you think?"

I frowned and shook my head. "No, Owen. I don't like that at all. I think you've got it wrong."

"Really? I thought...you just said...I'm so confused." He studied my face with careful concentration waiting for the punchline that he figured had to be coming.

I broke into a giggle, "It should be 'James Taylor' instead of 'Taylor James' for sure. My last name should go before yours, ladies first and all."

"James Taylor? Like the singer?" He laughed and continued through his amusement, "Whatever you want to name it, I'm all in!" Owen sealed the deal with a long-awaited kiss.

CHAPTER THIRTY-TWO

Journal Entry

Could this really happen? Could Owen and I actually team up and start our own company together? I never thought of it before today, but it actually makes perfect sense. I don't want to get ahead of myself here, but it could work. It could work well. And I'm here for it!

The only part about traveling for your job that most people complain about is leaving a significant other behind, if you have one, and the strain it can cause on your relationship. Joining forces would prevent that from happening to us, and it would be one less obstacle for us to face as we move forward. Dear God, let us be able to overcome the challenges that come our way.

Just like the pact that we made about staying friends even if our romantic relationship doesn't work out, we would have to agree not to let the company destroy what we have either. If at any point one or both of us feels that it's not working, we will have to be honest and do the right thing by separating professionally.

Hopefully, it'll never come to that, but it's wise to go into a deal with a clear head and guidelines to follow.

CHAPTER THIRTY-THREE

The day of the prom had arrived. Ashton was filled with both nervousness and excitement, the typical feelings that a teenager experiences when approaching a major event in their lives, but doubled. Not only had he been questioning his sexuality, but he still hadn't come out to our parents, which I knew was weighing on him.

Honestly, for as wonderfully messy as adolescence was supposed to be, I did not envy Ashton. I knew firsthand what it was like to struggle with debilitating anxiety from an early age, but I didn't have the background knowledge on what it felt like to be unsure of who I was and what I wanted. To be hiding that from every person in his life, including the two most important ones, must have been unbearable.

Ashton stared into the tall vertical hanging mirror on the wall in his bedroom, seemingly pumping himself up for prom night. I assured him that he looked absolutely dashing in his tuxedo and provided every ounce of encouragement I was capable of giving. He really was a very handsome young man, even if I was biased.

"You are going to have the best time! Just try to relax and

enjoy yourself and your date." I said to Ashton as he prepared to head downstairs for the obligatory pictures in front of the fireplace.

"Thanks! I really appreciate you, more than you know. It's so nice to have one person in my life I can confide in and go to for advice no matter what." Ashton said, wrapping me in a hug. "Let's go get these pictures over with!"

Mom was armed and ready with her camera, as Ashton walked down the stairs and into the foyer. I gave her the same eye rolling look I always gave her when she pulled that old, low-resolution iPhone 6 out. *No way are we taking family photos with that outdated device.* I came strapped.

"Sophia, let me get a few with my phone so I'll have them right away to post onto my Facebook page. Then we can switch to your camera, okay?" Mom asked me in a gentle and pleading tone I could never resist.

"Of course, Mom, whatever makes you happy. You take a few, and then my baby will take over." My camera was my baby, and I treated it as such.

Pictures at our house commenced, but Ashton still had another round at Faith's house with some of her friends and their dates. Her house apparently had a beautiful open circular staircase with a sparkling chandelier that photographed wonderfully as large groups descended from the top of the landing. If I were Faith, I would have wanted the prom pictures taken at my house as well.

Once all of the traditional poses were captured, the entire crew piled into the white limo that took the scenic route to the high school in an effort to give them more time to enjoy the ride and prepare for the night. Upon arrival, Ashton and friends were welcomed by various teachers that had volunteered for the event, and they then would be guided to the oversized gym to partake in the year's theme: Enchanted Forest.

My part in all of it was over, and all I had left to do was wait to hear how everything played out. There was always some kind of drama at prom. I just hoped Ashton would not be a part of it and that he simply allowed himself to have fun and enjoy his youth.

Thinking about my baby brother at his senior prom and how he would be graduating soon and then leaving for college in Tennessee made me think about my big brother out in California. I realized it had been a while since he and I Facetimed. It was 7:12 in Pennsylvania, making it 4:12 his time. He would probably still be at work, but I decided it was worth a shot.

The lovely sound of the Facetime ringing got me amped-up to see Oliver's mug. He picked up, and I screamed. *I miss him more than I thought I did.*

"Oli! You answered! How are you?"

"Soph! Of course, I did! I just got out of work actually. What's going on?" It was so good to hear his voice.

"You know how it is. Just living my best life over here." I said to Oliver very sarcastically. "Ashton went to his prom tonight! Can you believe that?"

"Did he really? I'm so proud of my little dude. Who's the lucky girl?" I remembered at that moment I was the only one in the James family, the only one at all, aside from maybe Riley, that knew the deal with Ashton.

"He asked a girl from school who's in one of his classes. Her name is Faith, and she's a total sweetheart. They should be arriving at the school as we speak. Send positive vibes his way, okay?"

"Definitely! I'll have to call him this weekend to find out how all of it went. Does he like this girl, or are they just friends?"

"He likes her. He was creative in the way that he asked her, and he has been looking forward to taking her ever since. I also sensed a little bit of nervousness, which confirms he thinks of her as more than a friend. How about you? Is your love life going well?"

"Chloe and I are in a great place. She really is the most fascinating woman I have ever dated. Nothing about the time we spend together is ever boring, nor the discussions we have. I believe she's the one."

"Oliver! Yay! I mean, I had a feeling at Christmas, but I've been waiting for you to say the words." My heart was so full for him now.

"Thanks, little sis, but do not start planning our wedding over there just yet. I still have to get a ring and...you know, propose..." he joked.

"Wait! Actually? You are doing this? Oh my gosh, Oli!"

"You cannot say a word to anyone. I want to tell everyone myself once I put together a plan of action and location, and I also have to ask her parents for their blessings first."

"I can keep it quiet. I'm pretty good at keeping secrets lately."

"Hmm...what does that mean, Soph? Who else are you keeping secrets for?"

"If I told you, it wouldn't be a secret anymore. Besides, I promised them just like I am promising you." This secret was Ashton's to share, when he was ready.

"Understood! Well, I'm glad you called. Your timing was perfect. I have to get going because I'm meeting Chloe for dinner, but I'll be in touch. Goodnight!"

"Night, Oli!" I felt goosebumps all over my body. He deserved all of the love in this world, and I was confident Chloe would give that to him.

I treaded slowly to the kitchen and opened the wine cabinet. I pulled out my favorite bottle of pinot and popped out the cork. I thought the events of the night required a celebration, even if I had to do it alone, since nobody else knew why I was so overjoyed. I removed a goblet from our shelf of glasses and proceeded to pour. Harley came over and sat gently at my feet as I took my first sip, and the juxtaposition of emotions did not escape me. I placed my glass down for a moment, to enable both of my hands to be free to hug all of her.

"Follow me to the living room, my girl. We can watch Netflix and snuggle on the couch." I stood up to retrieve my glass, and she walked a couple of paces behind me to the cozy sectional. I laid out a soft fleece blanket for her to get comfortable on, and I scrolled to find the best rom-com trending. Harley agreed with my selection, as she usually did, and she hopped up to nuzzle against my legs. *What am I going to do without her?*

Ashton got home earlier than expected. I heard his car pull up in the driveway and his steps as he walked to the front door. Harley perked up a little on the couch, as did I, and I could barely contain patience for how the night went.

"Hey! How was your night?" I called from my spot on the couch nestled under Harley.

He shut the door behind him and did not even turn the light on in the foyer before heading straight upstairs to his room.

What? No play by play? Harley curled back up and closed her eyes. A pit then formed in my stomach. I had the awful feeling the evening did not go the way Ashton had wanted it to.

CHAPTER THIRTY-FOUR

The morning after the senior prom was tense, at best. I knew something must have happened to upset Ashton, but he wasn't in the mood to spill, made quite apparent by his closed door and lack of response to my knocking. At breakfast, Mom and Dad walked into the kitchen as I was eating some oatmeal, and Ashton was silently making an omelet on the stove. It was coming. I knew they were going to ask him how his date with Faith went. I was really not awake enough yet for a complete meltdown. *Did Faith ditch him? Did he kiss her and realize he doesn't like girls at all? What the hell happened last night?*

"Ashton, did you have a nice time at prom? Did Faith?" Mom finally asked after five minutes of him not even looking in our direction.

Ashton did not respond and proceeded to shovel his ham, tomato, and cheese eggs into his mouth as an excuse not to speak.

"Bud, your mom is trying to talk to you. What's up?" Dad chimed in, sounding slightly annoyed.

"If you guys don't mind, I would really rather not discuss

the prom. Let's just say that there were some surprises, and I am still trying to process it all." He continued to look down at his plate, and as I watched him. I had a feeling if he actually were to make eye contact with any of us, he might break down altogether. He seemed so delicate in that moment that I just wanted to wrap my arms around him and tell him that regardless of how bad it seemed, it would pass. It always did. Instead, I kept to myself and allowed him some space, even though my body was fighting not to reach out to him.

"Well, maybe we can help you process," Mom said. "Was there a development with Faith? Did you realize you do not see her that way?"

"Mom, Faith is great, and I still like her. As far as I know, she had a nice time at the prom." This was not about Faith. Something else happened. I had to know.

"Ash, if everything is fine with Faith, then what's going on? Did something happen with another one of your friends? Did Riley go to the prom?" Ashton shifted uncomfortably at the mention of Riley's name, and my gut knew Ashton's mood must have been a result of an encounter with him.

Ashton braved a glance at each one of us, and then he went back to eating his breakfast. He definitely was not ready to share. I wanted to know if I could help, but I also thought he needed time to sort through it himself. Maybe he'd journal first or practice another one of his coping strategies, and I wanted to give him the space to do that. Maybe then he'd want to speak with me privately before sharing any of it with Mom and Dad – and I'd be there, whatever he needed, no matter what.

"We are here when you need to talk, honey," Mom told him and gave his hand a little pat. "You and Faith looked fantastic together by the way. I cannot wait to see how all of the other pictures turned out!"

"Thanks, Mom," Ashton said, and then he put his dishes in the sink and exited the kitchen without another word. I watched him go into the living room to find Harley. He took her up to his room, and I was hoping with the comfort of our sweet girl and the privacy to write, that he would chat with me once he was ready.

In the meantime, I had some real estate to look for. Owen and I had decided to take the leap and find a studio for our new business. He agreed with me that the name of our company sounded better with my last name before his last name. *James Taylor Photography...it did have an excellent ring to it.*

Owen had some local work to attend to this week, so I was taking on the duties of finding potential places for lease and lining up the appointments to tour them. It felt surreal that we were doing this, but it also simultaneously felt overdue for me.

I found a few that looked suitable and checked many of our boxes. I called to set up viewing times for when Owen and I could both go, and after I calmed down from the elation of actually having our own photography studio, I texted Owen to give him the news.

A few hours passed, and I heard the door to Ashton's bedroom open, and then Harley came out and walked down the stairs. When I didn't hear his door snap closed, I let Harley outside to do her business and then headed up to see how he was doing. When I got to his doorway, I saw him at his desk writing in his journal, and I knew that was a good sign. His face appeared somewhat relaxed.

"Hey, how's it going? Are you feeling any better?" I asked, praying I didn't sound too intrusive.

"You can come in. I'm okay." He put his pen between two pages and shut the journal.

"What has you in your head today? Is it Riley? Did you just not want to give me any details in front of Mom and Dad?"

"It is Riley. He went to the prom last night too, and I have to admit I was worried about him bringing a girl from our school or maybe a girl from another school. I would be lying if I said I didn't wonder about it, given our history."

"Was it the girl he brought that surprised you? Do you know her?" I was honestly very thrown off. Ashton had never mentioned liking another girl at school, so I didn't know how Riley bringing a particular girl to the prom would be confusing or upsetting.

"He didn't bring a girl to the prom; he just came with a couple of friends."

"So what's the problem then? Help me out here. What am I missing?"

"It isn't about who he showed up with. It's how he showed up. He came to the prom late...and was sort of...drunk. It was only obvious if you got within five feet of him, but I got really scared for him."

"Yikes! Did he get caught?"

"I didn't want him to get caught, so I asked him to go outside with me. He agreed to, and I grabbed some bottles of water on the way out of the gym. It got worse though." Ashton had a peculiar look on his face.

"It got worse than him showing up intoxicated to a school event? Students can get suspended for that, even told that they can't graduate. What was he thinking?"

"I'm not sure, but he came with two other senior boys, and he mentioned that he was at one of their houses, so I'm guessing that's where they had some alcohol before coming over. Apparently, they were contemplating skipping the whole thing and then changed their minds." Ashton was fidgeting nervously, picking at the skin around his fingernails while he spoke.

"Okay…we can talk more about that later, but what happened when you guys were outside talking?"

"Well, you know how we have been in the same therapy group at school, and you know how I told you he was going to share something with me the one day after our session?"

"Yeah, I remember that. The two of you were walking to your next class, and you thought maybe he was going to tell you why he was in counseling or why he freaked and ran out the night you kissed him, but the bell rang."

"Right! The bell rang, and I never got to hear what it was. There hasn't been a chance at school since to talk again alone either, until last night."

"He told you? What is it?" I needed to know now; I was invested.

"It was very confusing when he first started out, and it has been disconcerting ever since to be honest. I'm trying to dissect it all, but I am relieved he finally opened up."

"Absolutely! It's a shame he had to have alcohol in his system to feel comfortable enough to do so, and I really hope you were able to make sure he got home safely from the high school."

"I did. I offered a ride home to him and the other two guys. They were able to conceal their drunkenness from the chaperones somehow. I think the water helped a lot."

"Well, I'm glad he didn't get into a ton of trouble, even though it may have taught him a lesson. So, what did he share with you? You have me at the edge of my seat!"

"Well…the thing is…and you won't believe this, especially after everything…but, Soph…Riley told me he's gay. He is gay, and he's known for a few years, and he used to get bullied for it at his last school – that's why he left there, that's why he's in therapy, and that's why he hasn't *come out* here at all."

"Wow! That's a lot. I feel so bad that he had to go through that. People can be cruel and hateful, and it's not okay. On the bright side, I guess you were actually picking up on some kind of vibe from him after all. Even if he isn't into you like that, you had an intuition that he was interested in guys. At least, your gaydar is on point." I joked lightheartedly.

"Yeah, and he has been wanting to just finish his senior year in peace without anyone knowing. He was upset when I kissed him because he thought I figured him out and because I was the only friend he had made here."

"I have to say, Ash, I'm glad this is all out in the open. If anything, it provides a great deal of clarity. Now you know exactly where he's been coming from."

"True. It really does make me understand him more and the whole situation between the two of us." Ashton took a huge breath in and out, expressing a sigh of relief.

"Did you share anything with him about you going with Faith as your date and the bisexual stuff, or at least that you're still figuring some things out?" I heard the hardwood floor creak in the hallway outside of Ashton's bedroom. His head snapped toward the door, a wild look of panic igniting in his eyes.

"Mom! How long have you been standing there?" Ashton asked our mom, who was now standing in the doorway staring at us.

"Long enough to know you haven't been honest with us," Mom said, her expression unrevealing. I stepped aside and sat on the chair next to his bed.

Ashton jumped up from where he had been sitting and approached Mom. "I didn't want you to hear about it like this, and I'd really rather have this conversation with you and dad at the same time." Ashton maturely addressed Mom's reaction.

Mom's posture softened as she nodded, "That's fine, honey. I can see how that would be easier. Your father is down in the family room. How about you meet us down there in five minutes?" Mom compassionately composed herself.

"Alright, I'll be down soon. I want Sophia there too." Mom looked at me, and I wondered if she was grateful he had confided in me or jealous he had not confided in her. I gave her a reassuring smile, and she exited the room.

A few minutes later, Ashton and I joined our parents. Dad had this inquisitive facial expression, waiting to hear news that Mom must have said was coming. I sat next to Ashton on the couch to offer my support, and I nonverbally urged him to jump in.

"Mom and Dad, I have been wanting to speak with both of you for while now, but I haven't been ready, or...I wasn't sure how to initiate the conversation."

"Ashton, you can tell us anything. We are always here for you for whatever you need," Mom said.

"I appreciate that. I know neither one of you would be angry with me over this, but I suppose I've been apprehensive because I don't want to disappoint anyone, especially considering our religion, and the reality is I am trying to figure things out...you know, like find my place and find myself. Does that make sense?"

"Of course! We will support whatever it is that you're going through. What's been going on, and why is religion a factor here?" Dad asked.

"I don't know; some people judge others for being different from what is expected or accepted in the church. You know what I'm saying?"

"Ash, times have changed. It is much more common now for someone to walk down their own desired path, whether it be with sexuality or pre-marital sex," I said, wanting him to understand the evolution.

"I agree with your sister," Mom added. "Tell us what has been happening."

"Well...over the last year, I have been having these realizations about certain preferences I have when it comes to dating." Ashton glanced at me and then back to our parents on the adjacent couch. "It began when I met Riley."

"Did Riley make you realize that you maybe had interest in boys instead of girls?" Dad followed up.

"No...I still have interest in girls, Dad."

"You do? What happened with Riley then?"

"This is hard for me to explain, and I don't know that I'm doing the best job."

"Take your time, son," Mom encouraged him.

"When I met Riley and became close to him, I felt things that were super unfamiliar and confusing. I never had any attraction to a guy before him, and I didn't know what to think. It was all brand new territory."

"Were you and Riley seeing each other, in that way?" Dad asked Ashton with an open mind.

"I actually thought we might be, but when I showed him... well, when I sort of...um, when I tried to kiss him one night, he gave me the distinct impression that he didn't feel that way about me." Ashton fumbled through his story.

"Well, that had to be disheartening in the moment, I'm sure," Mom said.

"It was rough that night and for many weeks after. I've accepted that he doesn't feel that way about me though, and I've learned a lot about myself since."

"Can you tell us what you've learned, just so we can gain some insight about the journey you've been on?" I prompted Ashton to finish his explanation.

"Knowing I had a connection with Riley...that struck me as more than a friendship...brought awareness to my interest in guys. I hadn't ever known before I had any kind of attraction there. I only ever felt that way towards girls." Ashton took a deep breath and looked both of my parents in the eyes. "*Still* feel toward girls. It's a lot to process and can seem complicated, but I don't really date with gender in mind. For me, it's more about who the person is and how we relate to one another." The room was quiet for a few seconds, and then Mom broke the silence.

"So, you're saying that you're...bisexual then?" Mom asked with genuine curiosity. After the terse silence, the question struck me as so funny. Leave it to Mom to make sure she had all of the correct terminology. Ashton joined me in laughter, and then so did our parents. The moment sliced through whatever tension was left in the space, and instead we laughed ourselves to tears.

My parents reached out to give Ashton a hug, and our tears of laughter quickly shifted to tears of joy and relief.

My mom kissed the top of Ashton's head and brushed his hair back with her hand, like she used to do when we were little, "We love and support you, and we will *always* be here for you. That, my dear, is what family is all about," Mom said, as she pressed another kiss to his cheek.

CHAPTER THIRTY-FIVE

As much as I didn't want to believe it, Harley was getting worse. I knew I should be prepared to imagine my life without her in it, since I had known she was sick for some time now, but I was deeply struggling with that thought. *How will I ever say goodbye to her?* She was family. I woke up to her face every morning. I talked to her when I was sad and when I was happy. She knew all of my secrets, things I'd never told anyone. A life without Harley was a life without daily therapy and my much needed dose of unconditional love.

I still remembered driving to that farm out in Honey Brook to see her litter. I knew right away which puppy I wanted, but the decision was ultimately up to Mom and Dad. Harley did all of the right things on that day. She was calm and playful at the same time, kept a smile on her face, and nuzzled her way right into our hearts. How could we not take her home?

We got her into the car after settling everything with the breeder, and we all took turns holding her the whole drive back to Buckingham. She ended up throwing up on Oliver after about fifteen minutes in the car, and that may be one of the only times in her life I was thankful I hadn't been holding her. Luckily, he was wearing two shirts, so he was able to remove one in the hopes of not smelling like doggy vomit.

The rest of the ride was fairly smooth, aside from some minor whining – mostly from Ashton, who hated long car rides. Harley whined a little too. There were ten pups in her litter, and she stood out the most among the bunch. We wanted to give her a loving home, to offer her the best life we could, and she ended up making our lives better.

Fast forward to the present day, and I found myself at a pause, with no concept of contentment if she was not there. However, I watched her and heard her wheezing in discomfort, pacing more frequently than ever before. Though I'd hoped she might overcome this, I was starting to come to terms with the fact that I'd soon have to accept the opposite. Harley was the strongest, most persevering animal I had ever encountered, sometimes stronger than most humans I knew, and I believed she was trying to hang in there for us more than herself. She knew how much she was loved and the devastation that would be left behind in her absence.

Over the next week, we all worked hard to come to terms with the end of the road, the moment when Harley would cross over the rainbow bridge and become our forever guardian angel. Each day, I grew a touch closer to dealing with the insurmountable burden everyone in the James family would have to carry once she made her departure from this earth.

"I feel like we are down to our last day with our girl," I said to my dad as he was sitting on the couch in the family room with Harley in his lap asleep. Dad nodded in agreement and despair.

"Honey, I think…" his eyes brimmed with tears as he continued, "she may need us to tell her that it's okay for her to let go. She can see in our faces how hard we're all handling this. Please call your mom from downstairs and find out where

Ashton is for me. We should gather around her and make sure she understands that we'll help each other get through this." Dad shifted to kiss Harley on the forehead and pulled her up to his chest. My heart ached immeasurably.

Once the four of us were together, we surrounded Harley to reassure her that it was okay to stop fighting. Individually, we shared a favorite memory with her and let our girl know that she would always be in our hearts, that we would never stop thinking of her and talking about her, that her pictures would remain all over the house, and that she would always be a member of the James family.

At this point, Harley was having a hard time making it up the stairs to her usual sleeping spot in my bedroom, so I volunteered to sleep in the family room that night with her, feeling that she may not make it through until the next morning. Ashton said that he wanted to join me, at least for a while, and Mom and Dad headed to bed, giving Harley one last hug and kiss before doing so. I snuggled up on the couch alongside her, wrapped comfortably in her favorite pink fleece blanket. Ashton dozed off on the chair after petting her over a hundred times from the other end of the couch, and I fell asleep with sadness in my heart, but was comforted by the many memories I'd made with a dog who'd brought more love than I could've ever imagined.

When morning came, the sun broke through the slits between the blackout shades, and I opened my eyes with dread and hesitation. *What if she's gone?* I drew in a long deep breath, and I sat up to see Harley still laying on the couch with me under her blanket. She had not moved from that spot all night. I touched her fur and her face with adoration, thinking she had crossed over in her sleep. To my surprise, she was still breathing and even snoring a little. I leaned over to wake my brother.

"Ashton...Ash...wake up," I whisper yelled to him in hopes that I wouldn't disturb Harley. "Ash..."

Ashton turned to one side and then the other. He stretched his legs, opening his eyes to discover he was not in his own bed, and scanned the room in a daze. He then snapped to reality, landing his glance on the two of us.

"Soph, is she...is she still with us?" Ashton anxiously asked me to confirm her current state. I could tell he had the same fears.

"She is. She's breathing slowly, but she's still with us. Can you go up and wake Mom and Dad and let them know? I doubt she is going to make it through today. She has not moved since we all said goodnight."

Ashton went to get them, and I fetched my phone to try and capture a few photos of her, for what I could only assume would be our last day with her. I sent one to Owen and Rae first in a group chat with a text that reads: *This girl is a fighter.* Owen responded with a lot of heart emojis, and Rae responded with a heart and prayer emoji. They both asked if I needed anything. The truth was all I needed right now was to improve my level of acceptance.

Mom and Dad came down from their bedroom, joining Ashton and me with Harley. They assessed her breathing and lack of movement, and with a few gentle exchanges back and forth, they decided it was time. The last thing we wanted was for her to suffer in any way, and we could see that she was growing weaker with each passing moment.

"I'm going to call the vet and see if we can bring her over this morning. It wouldn't be fair to hang on any longer. It really is time for us to say goodbye." Dad told us with tears in his eyes, and we all agreed. I could barely hold it together, and I felt the floodgates opening up. My chest tightened, and I erupted into waves of heavy sobs. *My life will never be the same without her.*

When we reached the vet on the phone, they told us to bring her right over and that all four of us were welcome in the room. We quickly dressed and piled into Dad's Jeep with Harley laying on top of Ashton and me in the back, insisting we wanted to savor every last bit of cuddles we could before... well, before the inevitable moment we'd all been fearing actually happened.

Harley's doctor was waiting at the front door as we pulled up to the building. Dad lifted her out of the back seat, since she could no longer walk on her own, and carried her in. Mom brought the blanket and pillow Harley had been laying on all of the previous night, so she gathered those and took them in with us. At least, her final moments would be spent with items of comfort and familiar smells.

"All of you can sit wherever you like, even on the floor with Harley. It is very important she has her family here when she goes. Dogs will look for their owners, their loved ones, to know they are here for them and to know they are not alone." Dr. Stanmore said to us. "I am going to give her a needle, and about thirty seconds later, she will leave us. You may hear one deep breath after the injection, so do not be alarmed."

I sat on the floor, where Harley laid on the blanket and pillow from home. I positioned myself next to her with my right arm wrapped around her and my head near hers. Ashton sat on the opposite side, petting her head and ears. Mom and Dad were sitting on the couch a few feet away. I took several deep breaths in and out. My family did the same, as we could not bear what was about to happen.

"You will never know how much you will be missed," I whispered to her. She had lost the ability to look into my eyes, which made me even more emotional, but I was sure she understood every word I had said.

The doctor injected her with the needle, and I froze, holding onto her paw with my left hand. Thirty seconds passed in what seemed like a blink before Harley took her last breath and finally let go. Our girl was gone. I looked at my parents to see tears streaming down both of their faces. Ashton was latching onto her fur refusing to say goodbye. I continued to sob uncontrollably.

Her doctor stood up and left us to be alone with Harley, telling us to take all of the time we needed. Little did she know I needed way more time than what would be considered a normal amount at the veterinarian's office. I grabbed a pair of scissors from the counter in the room, snipped a few hairs off the end of her tail, placed them temporarily in a paper towel, and tucked the folded paper into my purse. My brother and parents regarded me warily; however, my actions felt warranted. I wanted to keep a piece of her with me forever. I hoped it would always smell like her, that it would always feel like her, and that it would always take me back to the good memories I had with her. I hoped...I just hoped this might be able to offer me some comfort while grieving.

Ashton finally removed himself from Harley and the floor, saying he needed to get out of there. I gave her one more hug and put my arms around my mom, who was completely beside herself.

Mom returned the hug and then quickly swiped at her eyes. Through a sniffle, she said, "Sophia, you and your father should go follow Ashton out. I need a minute alone with her."

We did what she requested and closed the door quietly behind us. Roughly ten minutes later, she emerged from the office, still using a well-worn tissue to dry her eyes. I was unsure of what she did or said while she was alone, but she would not have told us to go if she hadn't needed the time to herself. In my head, my mom was thanking Harley for all of the good times and asking her to watch over the entire James family. It was either that, or she also wanted a hair clipping. I smiled at the thought.

The receptionist gave Dad a form to fill out that specified exactly what our family would like in regards to the ashes, and it also asked if we would like a paw print of hers in clay included. We briefly discussed our options, and Dad signed off on having Harley's ashes be put into a wooden box for the mantle and a clay paw print with a prayer attached.

Once we left, there was still one thing left to do. The James family had a tradition of going to the prayer garden in our parish every time we lost a loved one, and there was no difference here. We parked and walked up to the angel statues. We stood close and began to pray. Even though Mom may have already mentioned this, I asked Harley to stay with us, to be our guardian angel, and to always make her presence felt.

———

Once we arrived back home, we mournfully dispersed throughout the house, not knowing what else to really say to one another. I also thought everyone, including me, just wanted to be alone with their thoughts. It had been a very mentally and emotionally exhausting experience, and it would take a lot of time to figure out ways to cope.

I walked to the family room to sit where she last was, to try and be close to her again. To the right of the couch where she'd been laying, I saw her dog bed with a couple of toys in it and her stuffed lion that she considered her baby. I took another deep breath in and out. I grabbed the bed, her lion, and the toys, and I walked down to the basement with them, not to erase her in any way, but rather to make things easier on all of us. I contemplated taking the lion up to my room and putting it in my bed, but ultimately decided it was probably not the healthiest of ways to make peace or attempt to move forward from this heartbreak.

While I was in the basement, the doorbell rang. As I climbed the stairs back up, I heard the sound of two male voices. I rushed up and opened the door. Upon seeing Owen, my eyes filled up again, and tears streamed down my face.

I rushed past my dad to give Owen a tight hug. "Hey, how are you holding up?" Owen asked as he returned the hug.

"I'm okay, I guess. We are all just trying to let it sink in. Thank you for coming over." I didn't want to let him go.

Dad handed me a tissue from the box on the small round table by the staircase, and then he put his hand on my shoulder.

"You know what I think is befitting for this occasion? A toast! Let's all go into the kitchen and make a toast to celebrate Harley's life."

"Say less!" I joked, pulling Owen toward the kitchen, and I actually smiled for the first time all day.

CHAPTER THIRTY-SIX

Journal Entry

S he's gone. She's really gone. No more slobbery kisses. No more waking up with hair in my mouth. No more. She crossed over and left behind years of memories.

I'll never forget the time I spent with Harley and what she did for my life. How could I? She was never registered as a therapy dog, but she was definitely my emotional support animal. I would have been lost without her, and I'm not exactly sure what I'll do now. Thank God for Owen being in my life.

I mean, my girlfriends and my family members always make me feel so loved, but Owen brings me this unique kind of happiness that I've never felt before. It's the kind where I feel like I'm capable of doing anything and handling anything, as long as I know he's on my side and that he'll be there for me.

That's how comforting and reliable Harley was. If I was going through something awful or stressful, I knew that all I had to do was snuggle with her, and I instantly felt better. She offered me unconditional love, and I'm so fortunate to have *known her. I'm thankful for all that she taught me through the years about the bond two souls can share and for the lesson she has taught me recently about how short life is.*

CHAPTER THIRTY-SEVEN

I t had been two weeks since Harley left us. Our family was not the same, and we never would be. We were slowly adjusting to life being different without her though. The only thing we could do was think about every treasurable moment we had with her and talk about them as often as we could. I looked at her picture on my nightstand before I fell asleep each night and told her that I loved her. I said a prayer once a week, asking her to continue watching over us and giving us signs that she was there. When I walked by her ashes, I grazed my hand along the top of the box as if I was petting her. Until I die, that dog will be a part of me, a part of the entire James family.

Everyone we were close to had been coming by the house or sending things over, calling, or reaching out in some way to express their condolences. She was loved by so many, and we were seeing how she touched their lives over the years. Owen, Raelyn, and Kendal had been kind enough to distract me and get me out of the house to pull my mind away from missing her. The three of them were the best girlfriends and boyfriend a person could have. It was like Dad always said, "If you were lucky enough to have a few people in this world you could count on and trust, you were unbelievably blessed."

———

This was going to be our first summer without Harley, and I needed to find things to look forward to if I had any hopes of staying in good spirits throughout my favorite season. The first item on the list was Ashton's high school graduation, a day that was expeditiously approaching and one he was over the moon about.

"Ashton, three more days! Are you sad it's all going to be over?" I asked him on the back patio as I brought out two coffee mugs filled with a steaming hot blonde roast. He liked to sit out there most mornings before school, which was so unlike me in high school – I used to sleep until the very last minute I could and then spent nearly an hour rushing around filled with anxiety about being late for first period.

"Sad? Sophia, do you know me but at all? Come on now. I am on cloud nine. Good riddance to that place!" He told me with the most delighted disposition, one I had not seen from him in a while.

"Well, I know you are happy to be moving on, but I want to make sure you don't have any loose ends to tie up before Friday. Do you have any counselors, principals, or teachers you want to speak to while you have the opportunity to do so? Maybe today you can stop and visit with them."

"Yeah, I do want to thank some of them for helping me, especially over this last year. I think I will start today. Thanks!" Ashton nodded and then took a sip of his coffee. I loved seeing him in this mood after everything he had been through these past ten months. "Having said that though, I think Friday's going to be one of the happiest days of my life! I can finally stop pretending for other people and spend more time figuring out who I want to be. College will be a whole different world."

"It definitely will be, especially for you. You'll be in another state at a large university, where you don't know anyone. Nobody will have background knowledge on you or what your life has been like, unless you choose to share it with them."

"I will know one person, Soph, but I'm not too worried about it. It's not like we will be rooming together or anything. He could end up in a totally separate dorm on the other side of the campus, and I may never even see him."

"Oh, that's right! You did say back in the fall that Riley is attending Belmont too, and I remember you feeling relieved that you had a friend moving out there with you." I wondered if he really was okay with Riley being there, now that they were not as close given recent events.

"He's the only person from this town I know of who's going there, and I'm thankful for that. Who knows, Soph? Maybe he and I can start fresh once we get away from this place and settle into a new environment. Although, I'm not overly optimistic."

I shrugged sympathetically. "You never know. I'm just so glad you're looking forward to the next chapter, whatever the outcome is between you and Riley. Nashville is such an amazing city with so much to do and see, and the southern lifestyle is one I can see fitting you well."

"I think so too." Ashton checked his smartwatch before grabbing his keys. "I should be getting off to school now. See you later tonight." Ashton handed me his coffee mug and hurried to the side gate of the yard to get to his car in the driveway. This kid was so grown up, and he was going to be eighteen soon, which was the second item on the list.

A high school graduation *and* an eighteenth birthday all in one week called for a fun night out. Mom and I decided to take Ashton out the night after he got his diploma, and everyone local was invited. It was a lot to ask for Oliver, Chloe, Paityn, Bradley, and Liam to come in from out of town for a one-night celebration. We planned instead to do Facetime with all of them at the graduation ceremony, at least for when Ashton was walking, and then a Zoom meeting the night of his big birthday. Owen had a shoot the evening of the dinner, so he wasn't able to attend, but he was coming to the house for the after party.

The next few days sped by before we could truly accept that my baby brother was no longer a baby. He was done. Graduation day was here. There was no going back. Ashton was thrilled, and we were thrilled for him. In two months, he would leave for Tennessee, and I would be left alone with my parents.

It didn't seem real. It felt like just yesterday that all of us were living at home, running into each other in the hallways and fighting over bathroom time. So many memories were made in this house as a family, and I could feel myself welling up with emotion just looking back on those times. Though I knew in my heart that change was good – hard, but good – it never made it any easier.

Ashton was only given five tickets for the graduation event, so he chose to give them to myself, Mom, Dad, Elijah, and Bethany. Our grandparents would have to hear the highlights at the celebratory dinner the following evening. Mom and I would of course take tons of photos to share with everyone, and I knew Paityn and Oliver would want to see as well. Mom would probably have them posted on her Facebook page before bedtime.

We met in the parking lot and walked over to the football stadium, where we found our seats about midway up the lower level of the home team section. Bethany, now six months pregnant, was grateful to not have to climb too high. We could not have her falling and risk hurting my new baby niece or herself. We squeezed in next to a family Dad knew, and they were armed with a megaphone. I gave my mom a wide-eyed look of panic that I hoped inferred: *This should be fun.*

Pomp and Circumstance began to play over the speakers, and the first boy and first girl took a step onto the track. The class always came out in alphabetical order, so we had time before Ashton walked. If I knew him well, and I was pretty sure I did, he was standing in line stressing out about having everyone in the stadium watch him as he walked from one side of the track to the other and receive his diploma up on stage. He did not like all eyes on him in any situation, not even one as triumphant as this one, not even when he had made this colossal achievement.

"Here he comes!" Mom said loud enough for all of us to hear.

I saw him at the opening of the gate next to his female counterpart. I had my camera ready. I zoomed in just in time to hear the principal announce "Ashton James" and watch him pump himself up to take the first step. He walked calmly down the track in strides, looking over to scan the crowd for us. We all waved and shouted his name, causing him just a tiny bit of positive embarrassment.

After all of the names were called, the students moved their tassels from the right side of their caps to the left side, and the ceremony came to a close with the entire class bouncing what seemed like forty beach balls to each other. Everyone then tossed their caps up into the air, with overwhelming pride.

After the ceremony, students and their families convened on the field to say one last goodbye and take pictures with each other. Even some teachers stuck around to wish the graduates well. Our group approached Ashton to find him giving another classmate a warm embrace. As we got closer, we realized it was Faith. She asked if I could get a few shots of them in their gowns. I agreed, of course, but they had to put their hats back on.

"Ash, are you two going to stay in touch?" I asked him once she had moved on to her family photos.

"Faith is going away to college as well, out in Colorado, so we will probably follow each other's lives on social media and text once in a while."

"Well, maybe when you both come home for holiday breaks, you can make plans to see each other," Mom suggested.

"Yeah...maybe...we'll see," Ashton shrugged.

The next evening, we all rendez-voused at Ashton's favorite restaurant, Enzo's, along with both sets of our grandparents. I had to admit I could never get enough Italian food, so I was very pleased with his pick. On any given Saturday night, this was one of the hottest spots in Buckingham.

" You did it, my guy! You must feel like a weight is off your shoulder," Elijah said to Ashton, giving him a playful punch. "I remember how good that day felt. It was so freeing."

"Yeah, it definitely doesn't suck," Ashton replied with a sly grin.

"Honey, we are so proud of you. You're all grown up now," Grandma James said from across the table.

"Well, I'm not a full adult yet. I still have to get through four years of college. However, turning eighteen in a few days has me feeling a little more mature. Wouldn't you say I'm more mature, Mom?" Ashton looked at the wine bottle and glasses sitting in front of both Mom and Dad's plates and then brought his glance back to her face.

"You're not that mature just yet, young man. A very miniature celebratory toast at home with us may be coming your way on your birthday though, if you behave yourself until then."

As far as I knew, Ashton had never even had a sip of alcohol, which was impressive, considering how high school kids tended to get into that kind of trouble pretty commonly. Even I had a taste of something here and there while I was a senior, and I was not exactly part of the popular crowd. Curiosity got the best of people sometimes.

"What about a cigar with these guys, Mom?" Ashton looked around the table at Dad, Elijah, and both of our grandpas.

"Your mother and I already agreed that would be alright, but only one, since this week is such a big deal!" Overprotective might be the word that sprung to mind when people thought of my parents, but they had done all that they could to keep us on a straight path from a young age, and I for one was grateful for that.

After dinner, everyone agreed to meet back at the house so the guys could have that celebratory cigar with Ashton, which would give us ladies a chance to gossip and catch up with Bethany about the pregnancy and pry for some baby name information.

Once Owen arrived, the guys headed straight to the backyard, as we poured some wine and gathered around the kitchen table, sparkling cider for Beth.

"Bethany, do you have a name picked out for my new great

granddaughter?" Grandma James asked within two minutes of taking our first sip.

"I knew someone would ask!" Bethany replied with a chuckle. "We do have some names we both like, but we want to decide once she's born and we can see her face to know which one fits her best. Plus, we aren't sharing the names with anyone yet."

It was a common Italian superstition that it was bad luck to name a baby before its birth. So between that and the fact that Bethany and Eli probably wanted to avoid the inevitable judgements and comments we were likely to make on the names they had selected, I kind of understood. It was worth a shot though. I supposed we would have to wait until September to find out once she arrived, which I was sure would be here before we knew it.

"Well, sweetie, we might have the urge to ask you every few weeks in hopes that you break, but I can totally respect you and Eli wanting to wait," Grandma said. "Whatever you name her will be perfect!" Our whole family was just tickled pink about the new arrival, no pun intended.

"Do you guys have the nursery all set up yet?" Mom asked, knowing we were throwing her a baby shower at the end of July. It was slightly obvious she was fishing to find out what they already had.

"Yes, actually! We have almost everything finished. We just have to add a rocking chair and some wall stencils."

"Don't go buying yourselves a rocking chair," I said and winked at both of my grandmas. They had already decided they wanted to buy that together. Our plan was to decorate it at the bridal shower for her to sit in while she was opening all of her gifts.

"I promise! Just please give me a tiny heads up about the shower, okay? I want to wear something cute." Bethany smirked and looked around the table.

"Deal!" We all nodded in unison.

"Refill, anyone?" I took it upon myself to give everyone a heavy pour.

The guys opened the back door that led into the kitchen, and they filed in, wreaking of cigar smoke. I would seriously never understand the appeal, but to each their own I supposed.

"Ashton, I hope you don't plan on having another one of those for a very long time," I said with a disgusted expression on my face, waving my hand in front of my face.

"I won't have one for a while, Soph...well...not until the baby comes. Am I right?" He elbowed Eli and chuckled. *Dear Lord.*

It was hard to believe that in less than two months this teenager transforming into a young man would be moving away to college and embarking on a new journey all of his own. One chapter was closing, and the next one was beginning.

CHAPTER THIRTY-EIGHT

"Mom, do you know where I put my Stetson hat? I thought it was up on the top shelf of my bedroom closet, but I can't find it." I called from my room, clothes strewn about and closet upside down.

"Sophia, I haven't touched it. Did you let anyone borrow it?" she called back.

"I definitely didn't. I wore it when we all went out to Montana West back in December. It *has* to be in this house somewhere." I continued to search.

"Check in all of the closets. I'm sure you probably put it in one of the other ones after that *night out*." Mom reminded me of the amazing time we all had that night, when Owen and I were still dancing around each other, both figuratively and literally.

I took my mom's advice and searched the hall closets, only to remember I had stashed it with my cowgirl boots in the back of my bedroom closet. The flashback came when I was reminiscing about getting into my pajamas and picturing

Owen's gorgeous face and how badly I had wanted to kiss him while we were doing a hoe-down.

I packed up my large black suitcase, filling every pocket efficiently, and carried it out to the driveway, cowgirl boots and hat all accounted for. Ashton was not taking a car to college for his freshman year, and even though he was driving with our parents to Tennessee, I promised him he could put one of his suitcases in my car. This left a tight space for Rae and Kendal's luggage, who I had invited along for a girls' trip.

Since they didn't live far from me, I picked them up. Ten hours was a long time to be in the car, but with two of the best travel companions I knew along for the ride, I was sure it would fly by. We actually had a lot to catch up on, and I was eager to find out how things were going with Kendal and Marcelo.

"Soph, how have things been going with Owen?" Kendal asked.

"It's going really well. We've been looking for a studio recently so we can officially work together as photography partners."

"Wow, that is so exciting! Where are you hoping to lease?"

"We are trying to find one in the area or within thirty minutes of Buckingham. Owen has an appointment tomorrow to check one out."

"Good luck! I'll send good vibes your way." Kendal put her hands together in a praying gesture.

"Speaking of vibes…Kendal, is anything heating up in your world?" I asked, not confident in my approach. She remained quiet for a moment, and I looked in the rearview mirror to read her face.

"Hey, what's up? Is it alright that I asked?" I said, still trying to assess her face, while simultaneously watching the road in front of me.

"Would you mind if we talk about this when we get to

Nashville? It's a topic I'd rather discuss face to face and maybe after I get some liquid courage," Kendal respectfully requested. To honor her wishes, we decided to put our favorite country station on Sirius radio for a while, and Kendal and Rae both fell asleep after a few hours. Once we stopped to use the bathroom, I asked Rae to switch spots with me and drive the rest of the way. I too needed to rest my eyes. Otherwise, I would be of no use to Ashton with helping him get his dorm room ready, and I definitely wouldn't make it out that night.

When we entered the town of Nashville, the girls asked me if they could go to the hotel without me to settle in and take a power nap while I went to Ashton's dorm to help him get everything into his room and set up. I dropped them off and then drove over to Belmont University to start carrying things in from my car. We all met Ashton's roommate and some other students from his hall. I joked with my brother that regardless of his preferences, he'd definitely have some eye candy, either way. He actually gave me a fist bump for that one. Once Mom and Dad began to get emotional while helping unpack, I decided to take my leave. They deserved some alone time with him anyway, and I did not want puffy eyes on my first night downtown.

"Ash, I'm going over to the hotel, but I'll call you tomorrow to make plans for some outings before we head home." I gave them all a hug and agreed to see them the next day.

Upon arriving at the hotel, I grabbed a coffee in the lobby. I needed a pick-me-up if I was going to last a few more hours.

The girls were doing a little pregame action when I walked into our room, so I knew I had to hurry up and get ready for the night in order to partake. All three of us brought along our cowgirl boots, and I had my hat to go with them. Kendal was really into trendy hair styles, so she never wore hats, and Raelyn wanted to buy one at a shop in town so that she could always say she got it there. I didn't blame her. I always collected special souvenirs when I traveled as reminders of my trips.

Our first stop was the Honky Tonk Corral, which had a cover band playing the newest country hits. The hostess sat us at a table right between the music and the bathroom. *Perfect!*

Once we had our drinks, Raelyn asked Kendal if she felt okay to share with us what had been going on with Marcelo. She said she would after she finished her Redbull and vodka. Rae and I looked at each other and telepathically came to the conclusion that whatever it was Kendal had to tell us had to be juicy.

"Alright, are you girls ready for it?" Kendal said as she placed her empty glass down on the table.

"Do tell!" I said as I took a sip.

"Well, I would say I have seen Marcelo about a dozen times since we first met back in the spring. Even that night, I thought he was charming and smart, and I've been super attracted to him."

"That all sounds great! So, what's the problem?" Rae asked.

"I feel bad because he works with your cousin, Soph." Kendal shifted her eyes to mine. "That's why I haven't said anything."

"You don't have to worry about that at all," I assured her. "Tell us what's going on."

"I know I can trust you...both of you. I just didn't want you to think that I'm a bad person," Kendal said.

"We're your friends, and we would never think that. What happened?" I said as I put my hand on top of hers.

"I don't know if it's going to work out with us." Kendal took a deep breath.

"Did he do something, or do you just feel like the two of you aren't the right fit?" Rae asked Kendal.

"Well...I..." Kendal was struggling. Sweat was forming on her forehead. "I am the one who did something. Don't judge me."

"We would never!" Rae exclaimed.

"Okay...here it goes." The waitress brought over another round, and Kendal asked for three shots of whiskey. "I hooked up with someone else!" She finally blurted out in embarrassment.

"You thought we would think less of you for that? Have you and Marc even said you were exclusive?" I asked her, feeling like I might be missing something.

"No, we never labeled ourselves as an official couple, but he told me he wasn't looking to talk to or see any other woman, and I may have given him the impression I was feeling that too. I didn't want to hurt him, so I let him think we were on the same page."

"When did you hook up with someone else? Was it more than once or just a one time deal?" Rae tried to help us get the full picture.

"It just happened once, recently actually, but I'm not even sure how I feel about this other guy either. What's wrong with me?"

"There's nothing wrong with you. You're maybe just not ready to be in a relationship, and that's okay. You don't have to be ashamed because you're playing the field. Not everyone finds their person at a young age and gets married. Some never do," I reasoned with her, adding in how I was twenty-six and not ready to get married and how Oli just met Chloe in his thirties. "You are twenty-five and want to have fun. Do you!"

"Thanks for understanding and for trying to normalize what I'm going through," Kendal laughed and let out a sigh of relief.

"It is normal," Rae affirmed, raising her voice over the band as the song got louder. "Maybe just be honest with Marcelo about where your head is and how you feel, especially if he's thinking you guys are exclusive."

"I know. You're right. I need to have a sit down with him and explain that I'm not ready for something serious. He's a nice guy, and I don't want to hurt him. I'm just not ready," she repeated.

A moment later, the waitress came by with our whiskey shots. We raised them high and toasted to living your life the way you want to. *Whew!* That one burned going down.

The three of us strutted out to the dance floor in front of the band and stayed there for about an hour, where a group of cowboys on a bachelor party attempted to pull us into their shenanigans. The music was loud, the energy was high, and we all danced the night away, enjoying being young and alive.

The next day, we explored some of the bars owned by current country and rock artists, one of which we chose to have a late lunch at with Ashton and our parents. When they arrived, we had already reserved a table for six and ordered strawberry lemonades for everyone, since it was only noon, and Ashton wasn't of legal age yet. Before we even placed our food orders, Ashton was telling us stories from the night before and the first morning in his dorm. Apparently, he met a lot of his hall mates and stayed up late getting to know them, and even had a surprise visitor.

"He came to visit you? What time was this?" I asked, looking only at Ashton. I figured Mom and Dad knew since they had picked him up and drove over to the restaurant together, but I wanted to hear it from him.

"It turns out Riley's dorm is right next to mine. He texted me last night asking which building and room I was in, so I told him, and then, this morning he stopped over to see me."

"That's awesome! It sounds like things are looking brighter for you and him. Do you think you'll see him a lot?" I really hoped they would be friends in college.

"Well, that's another thing. He asked if I had checked my courses yet because the rosters were posted Friday, and I hadn't. He showed me how to pull it up on my phone, and we saw that I have a Sociology class with him twice a week. Isn't that crazy?" Ashton was so charged up.

"That's fantastic!" I smiled so big that my face hurt.

"I love that you have a good friend here with you," Rae told him. "I was always afraid of going away to college too far out of fear of being alone."

"It's definitely been nerve-wracking, even though I've been wanting to escape our little town forever. Riley's the only other person from high school that moved here, so I'm glad we are on good terms now. I think we'll just be friends, but that's enough for me."

Ashton thanked all of us for being there with him on his first weekend away at college. Our parents reminded him of how fortunate he and the rest of us in the James family were that both they and our grandparents had been putting money away since birth for us for college. Dad was an only child, so we were the only grandchildren his parents had. They all started an account for Liam too, and my siblings and I contribute on his birthday every year. My family was against having student loan debt, if avoidable. They had even been strict on us about grades so that we could each earn a scholarship to aid in the tuition.

"Mom and Dad, I do appreciate that more than you know, and I'm going to get a work-study job here. I want to do all I can to help pay some of the costs."

I had to admire my brother for all that he had overcome, for the strength he had to relocate, and for the responsibility he was demonstrating. I don't think I was as brave or as mature at eighteen.

After leaving Ashton on campus, the next thing on the agenda was the Johnny Cash Museum, followed by the Country Music Hall Of Fame. We spent a combined time of three and a half hours reading and learning about songs and their writers, as well as checking out items that had been worn in the past for events or videos and instruments that had been played. All of it was fascinating, and it also took a lot out of us. By the time we had made our exit from the last exhibit, everyone was wiped and ready for a nap. I knew the night had more to offer, but I just wanted to relax at this point. *Maybe a quick siesta and then back at it! Maybe.*

Well, that didn't happen. Ashton spent the rest of the night trying to get things decorated and organized in his room. Mom and Dad went back to their hotel for dinner and were fast asleep before nine. Kendal, Raelyn, and I ordered room service, had some wine, put on a movie, and hopped into bed. I texted Owen for a bit and then passed out. *There's always tomorrow.*

Sunday was our final day in Nashville. We were driving

home Monday morning, so we had to make the last part of our adventure count. I woke up to hear Raelyn on the phone with Kevin, and it made me want to hear Owen's voice. I grabbed my cell to give him a ring.

"Hello," he answered with a pep in his step.

"I miss you. How'd you sleep?" I couldn't wait to see him when I got back to Buckingham.

"I slept alright, but it'll be better when you are closer," he said.

"We get home tomorrow evening, but I'm sure I'll be super tired from the drive, so let's make a plan for Tuesday, if you're free."

"That's perfect! I work tomorrow but have most of the day off Tuesday, so I'll see you then," Owen replied. "Actually, do you have a minute? I have to tell you about something."

"Of course, I do. What's up?" I asked mildly concerned.

"Well, I went to check out that studio yesterday, the one I had mentioned, but someone made an offer on it later in the afternoon. It doesn't look like we are getting that place. I'm sorry."

"Oh, okay...that's a bummer. It sounded like a really good fit for us. Did the agent mention any others on the market?" I was disappointed but tried to remain hopeful.

"I haven't heard of anything else listed, but I'll keep my eyes and ears open. Enjoy your last day and night. I'll talk to you tomorrow sometime." Owen and I hung up after a sweet goodbye, and I prayed that we would find something soon.

The three of us got all decked out for our last night in Nashville and made our way downtown again. We ended up on two different rooftop bars, and then decided to try a party wagon with a group of other wild ladies, which ended up being more fun than anyone had predicted. We toured the entire area and got back just in time for a pop-up concert at Margaritaville. A few hours later, with insanely full stomachs, we stumbled not-so-gracefully back to our hotel to try and pack up for the following day. *Nashville, you will be missed.*

CHAPTER THIRTY-NINE

A month had gone by, and I heard from Ashton every couple of days through text or video call. He was really growing accustomed to university life. His classes were interesting, and he and Riley were back to being good friends, just like I had wished for them. Paityn made a solo trip over to visit him the weekend after we were there, being so close by in Georgia, and he shared his story with her about being bisexual. He mentioned to me that he felt it was important to tell everyone in person, so we agreed to respect his choice and keep it to ourselves until he did. While there, the two of them made plans to come home once the baby was born.

Speaking of coming home for the birth of Elijah and Bethany's baby, Oliver booked a flight home too. The baby was due on September 25, so he flew in two days prior. Coincidentally, the same day he came home was the day Owen said he wanted to show me a studio he found online that boasted a great location. The timing wasn't great, but with the housing market as precarious as it was, we didn't have time to waste.

At the sound of a car horn beeping three times outside my bedroom window, I grabbed my things, booked it downstairs, and ran outside, locking the front door behind me. When I strapped myself into the passenger seat, I looked at Owen's glowing face and felt intense butterflies in my stomach.

"Where are we headed, babe?" I said to Owen once we were a few minutes from my house.

"You'll see. It's a surprise. You have to love it. Promise?" Owen seemed like he had all of his eggs in this particular basket, which made me even more curious.

"Well...we'll see..." I quipped back.

We pulled up to a small stone building in the borough of Doylestown. It had excellent curb appeal, and it only took us about fifteen minutes to get there. *I like it already*.

The closer we got to the building, the more my interest was piqued. It was landscaped beautifully, but the inside had to be just as aesthetically pleasing. A woman who went by the name of Grace met us at the door with a clipboard and some literature about the lease. We spoke in the foyer regarding the layout, and then the realtor took us on a tour. The walls were a neutral off white color with rich crown molding throughout. The floors were a dark hardwood, which contrasted the walls and made the space feel warm and professional. There was definitely enough space here to set up a studio and an office, along with an area for inside photo shoots.

"Are there other tenants on this property?" I asked, as I looked out a window and saw housing behind us.

Owen and Grace eyed each other conspiratorially. I could tell they had a secret, and I was bursting to know what was going on.

"Umm...what is going on?" I asked, unable to hide my suspicion.

"You like it, don't you? It's perfect, right?" Owen asked me, his expression beaming with excitement.

"I love it. You still haven't answered my question though."

"Do you remember our phone call while you were in Tennessee, where I told you that someone had made an offer on a place I went to see?"

"Yes, I remember. What about it?"

"Well...the offer that was made...it was me. I misled you in case it wasn't accepted, and I figured I could surprise you if it was. This is the place I went to see."

"Really? You made an offer on this place? And it was accepted? That's why we're here?" The questions were coming out faster than my mind was processing.

"Yes...to all of those! It gets better too. There's an apartment in the back."

"Wait! So the lease...it includes on-site living? What about your condo?" *What is even happening?*

"It does. And it's ours too, if we want it. My lease for the condo is up in a month anyway, and I haven't renewed it, so that's not an issue. All that's left to seal the deal is your approval. If you're on board, we go to settlement, and we can move in within a few weeks!"

Is this real? Breathe, Sophia!

"Yes! Yes! I'm on board. I love it. I love all of it." *Wow!*

"I had a feeling you might, Soph! Grace, you can draw up the documents now. Let us know the date and time to come and sign everything."

Walking back to the car, I was truly speechless. This was all I had dreamed of *and more*. I was not only going to work with the man I loved and respected, but we were moving in together. *How did I get here? Harley, is that you making this all happen for me? Are you hard at work already?*

"Did I do okay?" Owen asked as he reached across the car to put his right hand on my left thigh.

"You did better than okay. I love you so much," I said to him just before leaning over to kiss the right side of his face. "You are unbelievable, Owen."

At dinner with Mom, Dad, and Oliver, I broke the news that our parents were going to be full-time empty-nesters soon. They were all very happy for me, and to my surprise, Mom and Dad said they would probably do more traveling whenever they both could get time off from work. I suggested a trip out to Cali soon, which Oliver heavily supported.

I wasn't the only one who had something big to share. By the time we were clearing the dishes from dessert, someone else had made an announcement. *I knew it was coming.*

While the four of us sat at the dining room table, Mom asked Oli how his relationship with Chloe was moving along. At first, he joked about how he was still keeping his options open. Once he realized nobody found that too funny, he pulled his cell phone out of his pants pocket and began searching on the screen. I immediately got goosebumps. I thought back to our phone conversation on Ashton's prom night, where he told me that Chloe was the one.

"I ordered a ring!" Oliver said as he showed us his phone screen. It was a picture of a stunning two karat diamond platinum engagement ring.

"Oli! I'm so happy for you! That's exquisite!" I belted out.

"Oliver, I knew you had found the one when you brought her home at Christmas time," Mom said as she stared at the photo. Dad reached out for a hug.

"Speaking of Christmas time…I was thinking…I might bring her home with me again this year and ask her to marry me at the village in the gazebo in front of the tree. What do you all think?"

"I love it!" Mom cried. "What day are you thinking about?"

"Well, you know how a lot of people get a little deflated the day after Christmas because the big day is over? Well, I want to propose on that day, and then every year we will celebrate the day we got engaged on the twenty-sixth of December instead of being sad."

"I think that's a marvelous idea," Dad said.

"It's perfect, Oli!" I said to him and jumped into his arms.

"Thank you! The ring gets delivered in a few weeks, so I'll have to do a good job of hiding it until then, and I'll have to make sure she doesn't intercept the package and ruin the surprise, but I can't wait to ask her to be my wife."

I remember when Oliver had told us he wanted to move across the country, far away from our family and everything he knew. We were heartbroken at the thought of not having him near, but we tried to be supportive, knowing he'd have to find his own way regardless of the distance. Though it was hard then, my heart swelled with appreciation for how everything worked out just the way it was supposed to.

That night I had a dream that Bethany went into labor and spent three days in the hospital waiting for her baby girl to be born. I guess my anxiety got the better of me sometimes. I woke up wondering what Elijah and Bethany were going to name her. Bethany shared recently that they were giving the baby the middle name of Elizabeth to take a part of her first name, so whatever they came up with had to go nicely in front of Elizabeth James.

In the early afternoon, since it was a warm day, I put on my bathing suit and went for one last swim before we closed up the pool for the season. I did a few laps under the warm sun and then hopped onto our pineapple float. I laid there daydreaming about the upcoming bliss in our lives and hoping my sunscreen wasn't wearing off. As the water took me to the edge where the steps were, I heard some commotion coming from the house.

I got out and wrapped my towel around me, and then I walked in the back door to see my parents scrambling. Oliver was on his phone, pacing back and forth. "What's going on here? I heard shouting from outside," I asked.

"It's Bethany, sweetie. Her water just broke. We're trying to find everything we need for the hospital. Oli's been notifying all of your grandparents," Mom told me.

"Yay! A day early! Give me ten minutes to get dressed and do something with this wet hair." I ran up the stairs into my room, changed faster than I ever had in my whole life, brushed my hair, and twisted it up with a clip. I searched for some items I might need just in case we ended up being there overnight. *Cell, charger, hoodie, mints, neck pillow...check!* I threw everything into a large purse, grabbed my camera and case from my desk, and sprinted down to the foyer. It was GO time!

The four of us rode together in Mom's SUV, guesstimating labor time, weight, and inches. Mom drove, while Dad, Oli, and I sent text messages to Paityn and Ashton, as well as other family and close friends to let them know the baby was about to make her entrance into the world. Threads to Owen and to Raelyn and Kendal were a series of repeated baby girl emojis. *My niece is almost here!*

When we arrived at the hospital maternity ward in Doylestown, we saw Bethany's parents at the front desk. They were waiting for the room number, along with approval to go on up to the waiting area. We greeted them with emotional hugs and baby chatter until the receptionist was available to help us.

Our group found a cluster of seats together and saved some extras for when our grandparents and other family got there. Bethany did not have any siblings, but one of her grandmothers was on her way as well. Within an hour, the room was filled with eager beavers waiting for our baby girl to make her debut.

At one point, Elijah came to give us an update. "Everyone, get comfortable. We could be here all night," Eli said, addressing the waiting room.

"We'll be here, son. Let us know if you need anything," Dad said.

We ate snacks, drank coffee, played games on our phones, and made small talk with each other about how much Elijah and Bethany deserved this blessing. Owen offered to come to the hospital and wait with us, but I told him it'd be better to wait until after the baby was officially here.

Two hours later, Elijah came walking down the hall again. *This has to be it.* As he got closer, the exhaustion all over his face made him look so much older. Being a first time dad in the delivery room had to be stressful, but I couldn't help but notice how much more mature he seemed as he entered this next chapter of his life. We urged him to have a seat and drink some water.

"What's the status?" Grandpa James asked him.

"She's dilated seven centimeters now. The doctor says heavy contractions should be starting soon," Eli informed us. "I should get back in there."

"Just send us a text when she gets here!" I shouted to him as he was already heading back to their room.

"I'm going to run to the gift shop," Oliver said. "Soph, come with me?"

I sprang up to my feet and linked my arm through his in response. Even though we had given Bethany a lovely shower in the summer, it was still nice to celebrate the arrival of our newest James girl with super cute pink stuffed animals and bunches of confetti-filled balloons to commemorate the occasion.

Upon our return, we noticed members of our group were either growing antsy or falling asleep. We had been waiting for hours, and I wasn't sure how much more coffee I could consume without my heart exploding. I sat down next to my parents and pulled my gray neck pillow out of my purse. I positioned myself in the chair where I could doze off on my right side, inches away from Dad's shoulder. I knew if I fell over, he wouldn't mind. Within minutes, I was dreaming of my new photography studio with Owen and what it would be like to live with him and wake up next to him every morning.

Suddenly, I was shaken awake. "What time is it? How long have I been asleep?" I spat out and rubbed my eyes to see Elijah standing over us.

"She's here! The baby's here! I have a daughter!"

I jumped out of my seat. "Eli!!! Yay! Congratulations!!!" I screamed.

"Get over here, little brother!" Oli said, pulling Eli in for a tight hug.

"Honey, we are so happy!" Mom said, tears filling her eyes.

"When can we meet her?" Bethany's dad asked, his lips quivering.

"The doctor said we can have visitors soon, but it can't be all at once," Eli said to the room of us.

While we waited our turn, we sent texts and made calls, spreading the word. She still didn't have a name, at least that we knew of, but that would come next. We just wanted to let all of our loved ones know that this amazing baby girl was here, all seven pounds and four ounces of her.

"Beth, she's beautiful!" I said as I took her in my arms.

"She looks a lot like you," Oli told Bethany. "For her sake, you better pray it stays that way," he laughed, poking fun at Eli who sat on the opposite side of the bed.

"Really funny, Oli," Elijah said with sarcasm.

"Thank you, Sophia. We are so in love," Beth said.

"Can you two get Paityn and Ashton on a video call now?" Elijah asked.

I handed the baby back over to Bethany and got in touch with Paityn immediately. Oliver reached Ashton within minutes. We told them both we had someone very special for them to meet. Liam was there with Paityn when she answered the video call.

"Mommy, she here!" Liam exclaimed. "She here now! Look!"

"Yes, bud, she's here," Elijah told him. "This is your new cousin."

"How precious!" Paityn's twinkling eyes expressed admiration.

"Congratulations, Eli and Beth!" Ashton said. "So, what's her name?"

Ashton asked the question we had all been dying to know.

Elijah held Bethany's hand. "This is Hope."

EPILOGUE
HARLEY

It's true what they say about doggy heaven and the rainbow bridge. We run around in a glorious, carefree fashion, all day and all night, our health restored, frolicking through meadows and hills, feeling the breeze in our fur.

It was tough to leave my family, knowing how much they loved me and how much I meant to them. I held on as long as I could, I really did, with the mindset that each day would give them more time to accept that it was my time to go. I fought every ounce of that illness until it consumed me, and I did it for them.

I now spend each day watching over them, like the guardian angel they asked me to be. I know I have a very important job to do. I'm in charge of making sure baby Hope is well taken care of and that Ashton doesn't lose his way. Paityn is counting on me to help Liam reach his speech and language goals, while

Oliver relies on my subtle nudges to lock it down with the wife he deserves. Sophia, my dear Sophia, was always so special to me; her and I had a connection that could never be matched, and I will watch over her until the day she joins me here in the afterlife. As for mom and dad, (Daniel and Isabel, I mean, not my biological parents), it doesn't get any better. They gave me the most incredible home, where I always felt safe and cared for, and I send them signs often to let them know it is okay with me if they want to do that again for another lucky dog, but only if it's a retriever, of course.

I remember when the James family came to the farm that day. I knew that they were going to be my furever family the minute they approached my litter. It was the way they watched me, the way they held me, and the way they talked about how adorable I was. They weren't wrong either; I was pretty cute, and I knew just how to play it up with my soft whimpering and my sweet kisses. They fell for my act, hook, line, and sinker. Ten minutes with me, and they were signing the papers to take me home.

When we arrived back at the James household that first day, I knew I hit the jackpot. I walked in to see an orthopedic dog bed, giant food and water bowls, squeaky toys, a treat jar, a stuffed lion cub, and no other pets to steal all of the attention away from me. One by one, the clan picked me up and smothered me with affection. They rubbed my belly and fawned over me like I was the only animal in the world. My days of fighting over nine other pups just to get a drink were over.

. . .

Growing up with a family like that, where everyone treats you like a queen, makes you feel like nothing can touch you. I felt that way every day with them, every day that is until it happened. I knew something was wrong; I just didn't know what, and let me tell you, the news hit me just as hard as it hit them.

Once I realized I was on my way out, I decided it was time to start showing everyone the path they were meant to follow. And if they ever veer off course, I'll be right here to help put them back on track. To them, I was a huge part of their lives. For me, they were my whole life…and what a life it was.

  - *Harley Louise James*

REVIEW REQUEST

Dear Reader,

Reviews are like currency to any author – actually, even better! As they help to get our books noticed by even more readers, we would be so grateful if you would take a moment to review this book on Amazon, Goodreads, iBooks - wherever - and feel free to share it on social media!

We're not asking for any special favors – honest reviews would be perfect. They also don't need to be long or in-depth, just a few of your thoughts would be so appreciated.

Thank you greatly from the bottom of our hearts. For your time, for your support, and for being a part of our reading community. We couldn't do it without you – nor would we want to!

~ Our Firefly Hill Press Family

ABOUT THE AUTHOR

Nelianne Genner is a high school special education literature teacher, who loves to read and write. She spends a lot of time with her family and friends and uses her experiences and relationships as inspiration for her realistic fiction work. Nelianne has a strong passion for art, dance, film, and photography. She resides in Doylestown, Pennsylvania with her husband, Curt, her retrievers, Livy and Paisley, and her rabbit, Gatsby.

Reach out to her and say hello on Twitter, Instagram, through her email, or through Firefly Hill Press!

Email: nelianneteresa@gmail.com
www.fireflyhillpress.com

Printed in the United States of America

Firefly Hill Press, LLC
4387 W. Swamp Rd #565
Doylestown, PA 18902
www.fireflyhillpress.com
info@fireflyhillpress.com

Print ISBN: 9781945495380
E-Book ISBN: 9781945495601

Made in the USA
Middletown, DE
07 August 2022

70763244R00146